THE WONDER BRA YEARS

THE WONDER BRA YEARS

RACHEL FEGAN

FORESHORE | LONDON

Foreshore Publishing Limited |86-90 Paul Street London EC2A 4NE
Reg. No. 13358650
www.foreshorepublishing.com

Published in Great Britain in 2025
Copyright © Rachel Fegan 2025
Rachel Fegan asserts the moral right to be identified as the author of this
in accordance with the Copyright, Designs and Patents Act 1988.

A catalogue record for this book is available from the British Library
ISBN 978-1-0684467-8-8

This novel is entirely a work of fiction. The names, characters and incidents
portrayed in it are the work of the author's imagination.
Any resemblance to actual persons, living or dead, events or localities
is entirely coincidental.

All rights reserved. This book is sold subject to the condition that it
shall not, by way of trade or otherwise, be lent, re-sold, hired out, or
otherwise circulated without the publisher's prior consent in any form
of binding or cover other than that in which it is published and without
a similar condition, including this condition being imposed on the
subsequent purchaser.

Set in Sabon.
Typeset by Richard Powell
Printed and bound in Great Britain by 4Edge Ltd, Essex.

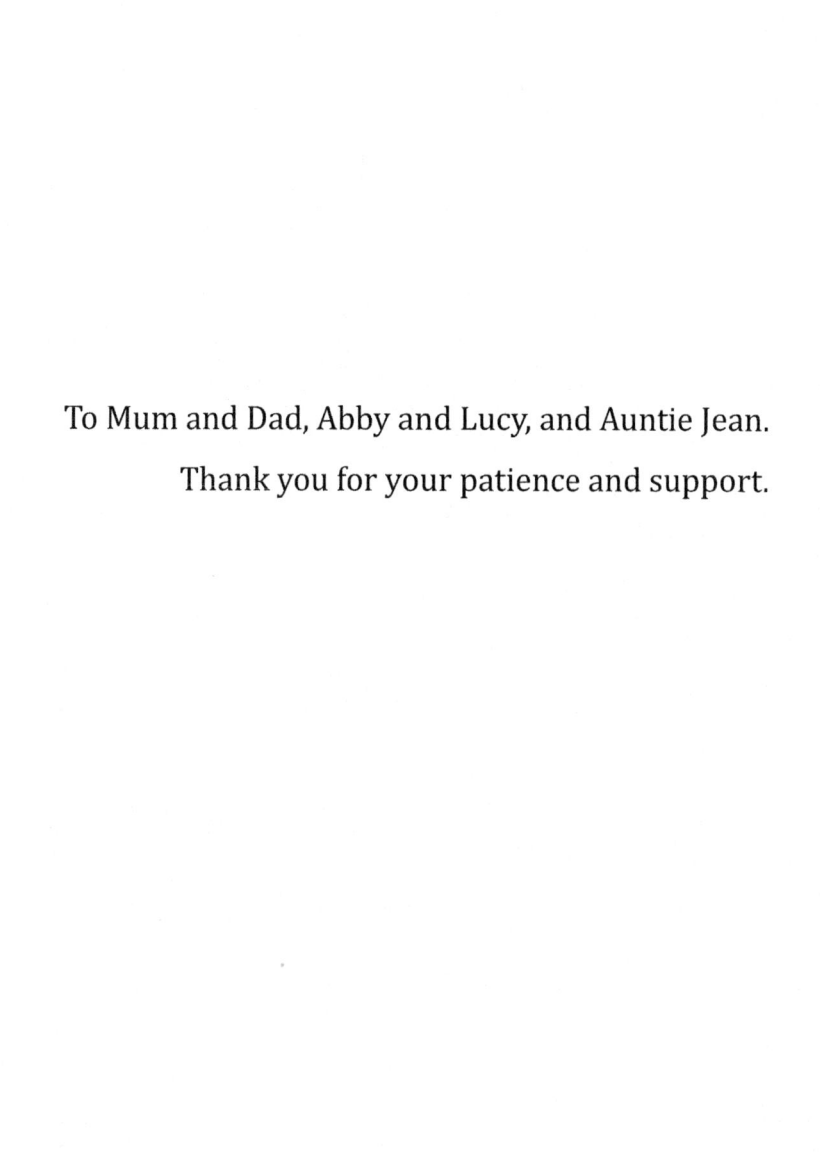

To Mum and Dad, Abby and Lucy, and Auntie Jean.
Thank you for your patience and support.

Chapter 1

IF YOU CAN imagine the Liverpudlian equivalent of Narnia, but no wardrobe involved! An icy cold blast from the North, the front door gap and a shiver from the East, the letter box with no brush. This was my current position, sitting on the bottom stair at home next to the phone table, willing the bloody thing to ring.

"Nicky, what are you doing?" I heard my mum's dulcet tones calling from the living room. If I'm not mistaken, I could hear the theme tune of Bullseye starting—the usual Sunday night television. I needed to hear the That's Life theme tune next, and then the usual Sunday evening dread would begin again.

I had been sitting on the bottom stair, reading one of my mum's magazines for at least half an hour. Before that, I was in my bedroom with the door open, keeping an ear out for the trill of the phone so I could run downstairs to answer it before my mum or dad did. So here it was, as expected. At least I had learnt how to re-pot plants and make a Chilli Con Carne now.

I was getting annoyed now and had slight frostbite on my fingers and toes. I dared not ask my dad to put the heating on; it wasn't worth the earache.

Why does a boy ask you for your phone number and promise to ring you at 6pm after football practice if he has no intention to? I know it was only 6.30pm, but being brought up with good manners, I wasn't happy. We met last night in The Hippodrome. We chatted for ages, having a brilliant laugh; we had the same sense of humour. His name was Paul. I was with my best friend Sharon. We were drunk before we had even got a taxi into town. As usual, we started our night in my bedroom with a bottle of QC sherry, R Whites lemonade, and ten Silk Cut. We always went out together and either started our night in mine or hers; either way, it involved sherry and Silk Cut. The taxi into town was always quite eventful, with us being loud, asking for the music to be higher up, and sometimes flirting with the driver.

I'd lost Sharon about half an hour before I met Paul. She went white, and when this happened, it meant she was going to be sick. So, it was my job as best friend to check on her in the toilets roughly half an hour later. I used to go after 15 minutes, but by then, she was fine and usually chatting with her new best friends, who she had met in the toilets.

"What's your name," Paul asked me. "Nicky," I replied in my smouldering voice, mostly gruff from too many cigarettes.

When I told him my name, he told me his sister was called Nicky, and so was his Auntie. This surely wasn't boding well for another family member called Nicky. We both loved the same TV and music. We danced for ages and then kissed! Quite a lot of kissing, hence the red chin this morning. Good old Sudocrem always does the trick.

The slow songs came on at the end of the night. He grabbed my hand and dragged me to the dancefloor, "Nothing Compares To You" By Sinead O'Connor was playing. We kissed again, looked at each other and giggled. I was planning our first date, holidays, marriage and babies! I always let my heart rule my head. And we definitely wouldn't call our daughter Nicky!

Before we knew it, the lights came on, and the bouncers started shouting, "Do your talking as you're walking," etc. I was more concerned about my smudged lipstick and frizzy hair from the heat in the club. I saw Sharon playing tonsil tennis with some guy across the room. As she came up for air, she saw me and gave me the thumbs up. Which meant I was okay with speaking tomorrow. I was secretly glad as I wanted to spend more time with Paul.

"I'll walk you to Chinatown and get some chips if you want?" I nodded in agreement and without speaking, as I did not want the night to end. He asked for my phone number before we left, but I didn't have a pen, and the rather rude barmaid said the bar was closed, even though I only wanted a pen. I searched my clutch bag and came across a slightly blunt eyeliner. I pulled a beermat apart and wrote my number. He folded it, smiled, and put it in his pocket.

I was 100% sure he would call. I would have bet money on it. Why? Maybe the numbers smudged on the mat in his pocket! Yes, that will be why, I'm sure of it.

Chapter 2

THIS LATEST LETDOWN seemed to be the norm for my love life. In other words, utter crap! I met someone, won them over with my amazing wit and personality, and then boom, there was absolutely nothing. If I had a pound for every boy I'd given my phone number to, I would be rich beyond my wildest dreams. I even wondered if it was because my name was Nicky, and he didn't want another family member with the same name!

I hated being tall. I was 5ft 8 at age 17 with a slim figure, long legs, amazing fashion sense - so I thought - but no boobs. Pamela Anderson was the pin-up girl, even though they were false. My friends were all smaller, petite with boobs. I was jealous. Surely the size of your boobs did not determine if you were decent girlfriend material? Did it? I was sick of being made to feel like the most special girl in the world for a few hours, and then the day after, feeling like I had two heads. I was so gullible, but I just wanted to be happy, and I thought having a loving boyfriend would do that.

It may be because I smoked. I was partial to a Silk Cut or two or ten. Maybe my breath smelt of cigarettes? I tried to disguise it with a Polo or Trebor mint. My friend used to always have Juicy Fruit chewing gum, but that was too fruity for me, and it went soggy in your mouth almost instantly. Never mind. I tried to forget this, but I had other things on my mind. Like my upcoming 18th birthday party. Some of my friends from school had already had their parties in local community centres or the upstairs of wine bars. I hated these family parties. The music was always cheesy, like Tina Turner's 'Simply the Best' and Stevie Wonder's 'Happy Birthday' and I hated this type of music. I liked Dance music mostly with the odd bit of cheese now and then.

My parents wanted me to have a party, but there was no way I had it in a Hall or Community Centre; I was petrified no one would turn up, the dance floor would be empty, and loads of sausage rolls and vol-au-vents left soggy on the buffet table at the end of the night. So, we compromised, and I agreed, but only if it was our house. You know, a small select few and not as much pressure.

"You only want me to have a party so you can show off your new G plan furniture and hostess trolley." Mum just looked at me with that look. You know that look that you daren't say anything back to.

So, the planning started. I wanted it to be cool, not embarrassing, which I suppose would not be too hard in a three-bedroom townhouse in the suburbs. However, I loved my home with my Mum and Dad. They were quite relaxed, considering they were in their 50s, and I had so much freedom for a teenage girl, even though I was partial to a Taboo and lemonade or anything I could get my hands on sometimes to get drunk with my friends. I still have nightmares about Martini and Crème De Menthe that I had stolen from the back of the drinks cabinet; it served me right, I suppose.

I'd been working in Labellos for a few months, and I had already made friends with some of the local people who worked in the designer clothes shops like Wade Smith, Drome and More Cherubs. I'd also made friends with some of the staff I worked with, and they turned out to be good friends even after a small amount of time. You just click with people sometimes without having to try.

It was late November when my parents and I came to an agreement that I could have the party at home. I understood their concerns about people drinking and dancing and obviously getting drunk in your home, but I repeatedly reassured them that the people I would be inviting would be on their best behaviour or else. However, there was a deciding factor that my Mum and I had witnessed, and we knew it would be something no one had ever seen at a house party before.

A month earlier, I had accompanied my Mum to one of her friend's 50th birthday parties at a labour club. It was the usual birthday party scenario, as I mentioned previously. However, the entertainment was something I had never witnessed before. We had a few drinks, and we felt a bit merry, and the atmosphere was as expected. Suddenly, the lights went down, and some form of military march music was playing. No one knew what was happening, and there were a lot of confused faces.

"Ladies and gentlemen, put your hands together for our act of the night."

The next minute, the lights were raised, and two middle-aged men with slightly rounded stomachs marched into the function room with no clothes on apart from a military-style helmet and a trio of balloons covering their front bits. They were both naked apart from the helmets on their heads, and three balloons at the front and absolutely nothing at the back, and I mean nothing. It was one of the funniest things I had ever seen, and looking at my Mum's laughter, I think she felt the same. We didn't know where to look.

The act went on for about ten minutes, and the atmosphere turned from mundane to electric. They took turns to burst each other's balloons, and every time one burst, the crowd let off an enormous cheer. When they left the room, the applause went on for ages. You would think Madonna had just finished a concert. It was at this point I looked at my Mum, and she looked at me and we seemed to read each other's minds. Call it mother-daughter telepathy.

Anyway, back to my 18th party. I was nervous as hell in the lead-up to it. My Mum and Dad had borrowed a friend's card for Macro wholesalers to get beers and wine. My Mum was an amazing cook, so she made chilli con carne and rice, curry, and the usual sandwiches. I wonder if she had got the recipe from the magazine I was reading.

The invitation list was not massive. The usual family members and then my close friends, a boy I'd been snogging recently on a few occasions and then my new friends from Labellos, who were great fun and had the party spirit running through their veins. And obviously the neighbours, so they couldn't complain about any noise.

I'd bought my outfit a few weeks before from a shop In Cavern Walks. It was a John Richmond Destroy bodysuit in iridescent purple and pink colours with a pair of crocodile print tight black trousers. I had loads of black heels, so I had no need to buy any, or should I say my parents didn't. I had gotten used to designer brands since I started working at Labellos, so they were too scared to ask about the price of things. If my Mum had asked, I would have told her about £19.99 in the sale. It was always the same amount, and she was always amazed at my skill in finding bargains. If only she knew there was probably another £50 at least to add to that.

The party was on a Friday night. Family and close friends had been invited about a month before, and then my new work colleagues, well, the ones who could get the night off. I'd made close friends with a few, so I mentioned to the manager a few weeks before asking him if he could give them the night off. He laughed when I asked him. "Where's my Invitation?" I laughed nervously. I told him he was welcome; he was alright, to be honest, but when your boss is in attendance, you cannot relax. He assured me he would do what he could. I told him to tell anyone to come after work, seeing as the last order was 11pm, and if it was quiet, we would start the clean down, etc., well before that time.

I was at work the night before, and some of the girls who had Friday night off who were on my shift were so excited, asking me what the dress code was, etc., and also trying to get information from me about a surprise guest that I had told people on their invitation. I was getting dressed up, so I said the code was dressy, but they could wear what they wanted as long as they turned up. "Don't be late, and don't be too drunk," I warned them, sarcastically with a smile. I wasn't really bothered, to be honest. If it were me, I'd definitely be a bit merry, and I'd want to be dressed up because if the party was crap, I'd be going to town after the party for the last couple of hours.

When we finished cleaning up, my friend offered to give me a lift home. I was so relieved as I was exhausted, but I had a sneaky feeling she just wanted the gossip about who the surprise guest was. I was onto her game straight away. I was dying to tell someone, but my Mum had sworn me to secrecy; even my Dad did not know - he was just paying for it.

Chapter 3

I WOKE UP fresh as a daisy. I got home just after midnight last night after an in-depth interrogation about the party and, what was planned, and especially who the surprise guest was. I was starting to panic now. I hope everyone liked the surprise we had planned and it wasn't a total letdown. My nerves were shot, and I felt a bit sick.

I went downstairs, and there was no one to be found apart from the dog waiting to be fed as usual.

There were some changes. The sofas had been moved, and the conservatory table had been moved to one side with a paper tablecloth placed over the top. On the kitchen side were wine and half-pint glasses, which were washed and placed neatly in rows. Then, the paper plates with serviettes intertwined with each other. The Hostess trolley was also out in its full glory, ready for the chilli and curry, I presumed. Every time my mum mentioned her hostess trolley, I would snigger at the Victoria Wood song. If you know, you know. Hyacinth Bucket sprung to mind, too.

"Mum, Dad," I shouted, but no answer. I presumed they must be getting some last-minute bits. The next minute, I heard the front door open, and the dog started barking. There were raised voices between my mum and Dad. I rushed to the front door to see my Dad carrying boxes of lager and my mum following behind with a catering pack of bread rolls, boxes of crisps and various other things wrapped up in catering packaging. Yes, I was right: another trip to Macro using their friend's business card.

I offered my services, but if I knew my mum as well as I thought, I knew I would get in her way, but I offered anyway just so she knew I cared - I more than cared! I was absolutely shitting myself, but I was grateful for all the effort they had put into my night. The party was due to start around 7pm, and I started panicking about almost everything. Would people turn up? Would people like it? Would anybody be sick on the carpet or drop a cigarette into my Dad's prized pot plants? He's read that magazine as well, I'm sure. I went to a house party last year, and my friend was sick on the pet poodle. Apparently, its white fur was stained orange for over a week.

The close family were coming earlier than everyone else, and my friends were given strict instructions to arrive no later than 8pm, or I'd kick off. I was so nervous. Imagine what I would have been like if the party had been in a function room. I probably would have fainted by now or left the country.

Time was ticking, and before long, It was nearly 5pm, so I decided to jump in the shower and start the transformation from hobo to honey. I grabbed my Timotei shampoo and conditioner and my Lady Shave and locked myself in the bathroom. I sat on the closed toilet seat and had a few moments to think. I was dying to light a sneaky fag and blow the smoke out the bathroom window, but I really didn't have the time. Let's get this show on the road, I thought to myself. I was pottering in the shower when, all of a sudden, there was an almighty bang on the bathroom door. My mum needed her shower and I could tell she was all of a tizz! I hurried myself along and appeared a few minutes later, flushed from the hot water and with a head of hair like Medusa. Natural curls were a curse to me. As soon as I got back into my room I plugged my old faithful BaByliss hair straighteners in because they took about 45 minutes to reach the heat I needed to tame these darn curls. I had a perm in the '80s, and I swear this had made them worse. God knows why I had it done, even permed my fringe! Dreadful, I still cannot look at photographs of me from this time. Think orphan Annie but blond, and you get the picture.

I did my usual beauty regime and then started drying my hair. I could smell burning! Shit! The straighteners were burning the carpet. Wow, for once, they have actually heated up properly. I acted quickly to start straightening my hair, and for once, it actually turned out ok. No need to get the iron and ironing board out for once. My poor Dad has had to help me with this on numerous occasions with a piece of The Liverpool Echo onto my hair before the iron was used.

I glanced at my watch, 6.30pm. My Dad had warned me to be ready at least ten minutes before the start of the party, even though people never turned up at the actual start time. I was on schedule with hair, so now makeup, which never took long as I was rubbish at it. Bronzer, mascara, lipstick that was it, and a squirt of perfume. I decided on Obsession tonight.

"Nicky, you better get down here asap," Dad's dulcet tones bellowed up the stairs.

"Coming," I replied, even though I wasn't. I could tell he was on edge.

"Knock, knock," on my bedroom door. "Ok, I'm coming. Bloody hell!" I charged towards my bedroom door, about to kick off. I was dressed and ready and it was only 6.45pm. I opened it, and my mum was standing there with a glass of Bucks Fizz in a plastic flute. We looked at each other and laughed.

"Come on, you get downstairs and have a look before your father has a wobbler." I grabbed my lipstick, did one more big squirt of perfume and headed downstairs. Here goes, I thought.

Chapter 4

I WALKED DOWN the stairs cautiously in my kitten heels, making sure I didn't fall. I had a cheek wearing kitten heels the size of my feet. My mum went first, and the main hall lights were off, but there were small lights twinkling all down the hall and on the porch. I assumed the Christmas tree lights were out of the loft! They looked amazing, although some of the lights were not working. Never mind, I could see the love and affection that had gone into making my night special even before I had come down the stairs fully.

I tottered down the remaining few stairs and walked into the living room, which was as bright and sparkling as the hallway. As stated before, the furniture that could be moved to the side had been small coffee tables adorned with tablecloths and a Kodak disposable camera on each. I was taken aback by this. I would never have thought of that. Full points to Mother!

I looked at the wall clock; it was 7pm on the dot. Oh, shit, here goes; I hope everyone turns up. Surely they would, wouldn't they?

I was guided into the conservatory to see the rows of Charlemagne fake champagne, cans of lager, Vodka, Bacardi and the usual lemonade, Coca-Cola and fresh orange juice cartons. Next to this were plastic flutes and half-pint glasses. And then I laughed. A small glass with paper umbrellas and a jar of maraschino cherries. So Del Boy but brilliant. Mange Tout

The front doorbell suddenly chimed! Shit, someone is here. I heard my mum running to open it. It was Grandad. He only lived up the road, Number 10. As he walked in, I saw my Auntie and Uncle follow behind; they lived at Number 131. It sounds mad that most of my family lived on one road, but it was all I had ever known. Like the Mafia, but no guns. They were ushered into the living room after Mum had taken their coats, threw them into my arms, and pointed upstairs. I assumed she meant to place them on her bed. I did as I was told and threw them on. I did not even look to see if they had made the bed; I just launched them.

I went back downstairs. By this time, there was music playing. My Now That's What I Call Music CD, if I'm not mistaken. The family were all standing together praising my mum and dad on their party decorations with a plastic flute of pretend champagne in hand.

We started chatting, and I was handed some cards and some presents. I was dying to open the cards to see what money was in them, but I was given a look and told to put them on the small table in the corner, which was the designated gift table. I suppose it was something to look forward to later or tomorrow.

Another knock at the door. It was Sharon and her Mum. My best friend. I ran to her, and we cuddled, both commenting on our outfits as usual, and her mum handed me a card and another present for the table. I could tell I had a couple of plastic 18th keys in gift boxes and a wine glass embossed with 18 today. "Use the glass tonight, Nicky," I was ordered by Sharon as she sniggered. I gave her a look, opened the plastic wrapper, and gave it a swill in the sink in the conservatory. Suppose it adds to the occasion, I thought to myself. I'll probably smash it in about an hour.

Before I knew it, the door was knocking, knocking constantly. Eventually, my mum just left it open. Our dog Sally would not run out. She just had a little bark. She was so good; she loved the attention and tummy tickles and I knew she would keep her eyes out for any of the buffet that ended up on the floor. "She won't bite," I had to repeat about a hundred times. Some of the neighbours seemed uneasy because a large black Alsatian cross collie jumped up at them to say hello. What I really wanted to say was, "Don't be pathetic; you see her every day sitting outside the house, and just because you've got some sequins on, you think you're Joan Collins." I'm the only Diva in the building tonight, and I giggled to myself!

We had only invited the neighbours just in case the music was too loud and someone vomited on their prize rose bush in their front garden. They cannot say anything really about whether they have been fed and watered, Mum always said. She was right yet again.

"Hello, thank you for coming," I repeated like Metal Mickey! It was just after 8.15 pm, and so far, I had counted six plastic 18 keys in a pink satin box. Seriously, what am I going to do with these? I just hoped there was a nice crisp £10 note in the card, too. God, I sound awful, but I know everyone else would think exactly the same. Wouldn't they?

I was chatting away to everyone, trying to mingle the best I could. The living room was nearly full, so I felt a bit better. Still no sign of the girls from work or some of my previous romantic acquaintances, and it was nearly 9pm. There was no point in me phoning them at home as they would be out and on their way, hopefully.

I had turned the music up so it was a bit louder, and I was busy chatting to everyone and feeling a bit drunk. The family members had moved into the conservatory, where there was seating. I didn't want to sit down and never did on a night out; I was scared of missing any action.

The next minute, I heard a scream, and the girls from Labellos had arrived, as well as a few of the lads who worked in a local bar and the bouncers from the Irish Bar over the road who always came in for a drink before their shift started. I fancied one of them. I think his name was Dominic, but I wasn't sure and didn't really care. He was the stereotypical tall, dark, handsome and dead good to look at when I was bored. I'd never even spoken to him; I was always too shy. My new party guests were all visibly drunk, holding cards, a bottle of Smirnoff, and an empty glass they had obviously taken from the bar they had been in before coming here and screaming to make their arrival even more noticeable. It was like a herd of glamorous size 8-10 elephants coming in with high-pitched voices, almost like a mating call on a David Attenborough documentary. Dominic leaned towards me and kissed my cheek. "Happy birthday, Louise," he whispered in my ear. Who's Louise, I thought? Aw, well, never mind. He's probably a sandwich short of a picnic, as my mother would say, but he still looked good. Sammy was one of the girls I was probably closest to. She looked gorgeous in a Vivienne Westwood Bustier and pencil skirt. She was the first to come to me. We hugged and kissed and got lipstick on each other's cheeks whilst looking up and down at each other's outfit choices.

"Is that a Westwood" I gasped in utter jealousy as her breasts collapsed over the top. I could never wear that. I would need scaffolding never mind a Wonder Bra. "What do you think" she smirked as she did a twirl. "And I got 20% discount." She looked amazing.

My family and other guests had noticed the new arrivals and were speechless looking at them and their outfits especially the older ones . They looked them up and down and commented how high the shoes were and they will probably break their neck. Sammy's bustier also had my neighbour Bill's attention as they were practically popping out. They were the life and soul of any party and it seems like they were definitely going to do the same tonight. Definitely for Bill anyway.

Chapter 5

THE MUSIC GOT louder, and people were dancing in the living room. My Dad kept turning it down, but this was pointless as I just turned it back up every time he turned his back. Sally, the dog, was ushered away several times by various people. She was totally harmless just after the sausage rolls.

Everyone kept mentioning the surprise that I told everyone about who was invited. Shit! I totally forgot about this. Luckily, my mum hadn't, as I was about to find out. I was socialising with all my guests, dancing and drinking; by now, it looked like a proper house party. Then suddenly, my mum approached me, grabbed my arm, and pulled me away towards the hallway. "They're here!"

"Who?" I asked, staring confusedly at her face.

"The Helmet Brothers. They are in your bedroom."

Shit, I'd forgot. Mum ushered me upstairs, and we came across quite a site! Here's the birthday girl. I heard a voice with a warm, friendly scouse accent. It was Jimmy, one of the infamous Helmet Brothers. Joey, his brother, just gave me a salute in character as his helmet and moustache were already in place. I had no idea they had even arrived. Super Mum, as always, had been on pins waiting for them and taking care of their discreet arrival. They were dressed as I had remembered. Naked apart from three balloons covering their willies and a military-style helmet with a small pretend moustache. I was speechless as I saw them; this was so different from the usual party entertainment you see anywhere, let alone in someone's house.

"Thank you so much for coming," I said and I hugged them both, being extra careful not to burst any balloons. Most awkward and tricky hug ever. We all laughed at the same time. It was so funny and surreal.

Jimmy handed me a tape cassette. This was their introduction and routine music. "Girl, go downstairs and put side A of this tape on when your mum gives you the signal"

Oh shit, I was rubbish at instructions, especially today, as I was drunk already. I looked at the tape and then looked at Mum. We both did that telepathy thing again and giggled. Even my Dad had no idea about this. I had to now put my youth theatre face on and announce the surprise downstairs. I just hoped everyone liked it as much as we did.

I shook my head, gave them a jokey salute, and made my way back downstairs. By this time, the kitten heels had been launched into the cupboard under the stairs, so I had a much easier exit than previously. He had also told me to get everyone ready downstairs at the far end of the room if possible and make the introduction, get them to clap, and press play on the tape when my mum gave me a signal to press play.

I hadn't even told Sharon about this. There were people in the living room and conservatory. It was pretty full now; most people had arrived apart from a few, and the atmosphere was good as most had a few drinks inside them. I headed towards the Hi-Fi system and switched the CD mode to tape. It didn't have the desired effect of quietness, so I had to make an announcement, even though I did not want to.

"Excuse me, everyone," I started. No one paid any attention. "Oi," I shouted in my usual dulcet tone. Thank you so much to you all for coming and thank you for all my cards and presents. As I talked, I tried to insert the tape into the cassette player, ensuring it was the right way round. No one took a blind bit of notice of me. They will soon, I thought. Then my mum hung her head over the stairs and gave me a thumbs up. I assumed this was the signal, seeing as we hadn't discussed the actual signal. Oh, bloody hell, I thought. I felt sober again.

"Oi!" I shouted with gusto again. "I'd like you to meet my special guests." Everyone soon turned round and I pressed play on the tape cassette.

The music started after a few seconds that felt like a lifetime. I made sure the volume was up, and then military-style march music sounded throughout the downstairs rooms. It started off quiet, then got louder. I was told to open the living room door and make a space before the fireplace. The marching music got louder, and then Mum appeared to be laughing and moving towards the conservatory. She headed towards my Dad, who didn't have a clue about what was going on. Also, I think it was to ensure he had the video camera ready.

The next minute, two men started to march downstairs and into the hallway and into the living room single file. Jimmy and Joey were about to appear to my guests, and I couldn't wait to see everyone's reaction.

The first face I remember seeing was Sharon. She stared and spat out whatever drink was in her mouth; I just hoped it wasn't red wine on the carpet. She looked at me and gave me the look we knew between us. The look that meant, 'Oh bloody hell, Nicky'. As the brothers arrived at the living room entrance, all I could hear was an eruption of laughter from everyone and a few looks of disbelief from a few, mainly my older family members, who had probably never seen anything like this before. I was trying to locate my Dad. I quickly found him with a smirk, holding the video camera. He was probably thinking, 'Jesus, what have these two done now'.

The dance progressed nicely, and the laughter surrounding them got louder and louder. The odd peek of a bum cheek or two was to blame, especially as they were quite unfirm and full of wrinkles, but that's what made it entertaining. I cannot stand those Chippendale-type strippers with the baby oil. Gross.

Sammy grabbed me from behind. "Nicky, you're hilarious; what happened to a magician or a comedian at a party."

"Paul Daniels was busy," I replied as we both burst into laughter.

All of a sudden, pop, one balloon at the front of each burst, leaving only two full balloons shielding their modesty. The faces of some of the older guests were a picture, and an almighty cheer filled the living room. I'm sure some of the older women made their way to the front of the small crowd. They were trying to look shocked but secretly to get a closer look. Next thing another pop. The crowd erupted into another enormous cheer.

The Wonder Bra Years

I tried to remember the first time I had seen them, but I could not remember if they got down to no balloons. I didn't have to wait long as there was another pop and raucous cheer. I'd got my answer. No balloons and willies galore. It was brilliant. Every minute of it was terrific, and so thought my guests by the looks on their faces. The round of applause at the end was deafening and seemed to go on forever.

Jimmy and Joey seemed to bow a hundred times while trying to preserve their modesty, but they did a little show and tell at the end. It was so funny, even my Grandad was laughing.

They then made their way back upstairs and got dressed. I followed them up a few minutes later with my mum and Dad to say thank you and offer to stay and have a drink with us and pay for them. They politely declined, as they had another gig in Ormskirk in about an hour. They gave me some business cards, though, and asked me to hand them out, handy as I'd already been asked by a few of my guests for their details. I hope they get loads of bookings; I'm sure they will.

After we said our goodbyes at the front door, I went back into the party and put the next CD on to get the party going again and get myself another drink. Everyone kept coming up to Mum and me and congratulating us on such a brilliant surprise. I was thrilled to bits. People talked about this for months, and it was my 18th party. My Dad grabbed me on the way back in.

"So, this was your secret with your mother. It was great love, and all your friends seemed lovely as he kissed my cheek with affection. There is no rush for them to go home, but keep the noise down, eh."

He hugged me and squeezed me. I couldn't wish for anything else, apart from Patrick Swayze turning up, but that wasn't going to happen.

Chapter 6

THE DRINKS KEPT flowing, and the music got louder for the next few hours. The atmosphere was electric; everyone was dancing and chatting. Bill, the neighbour, even got Sammy dancing, but it was obvious he just wanted to inspect the bustier a bit closer. She was winding him up, twirling him around, etc. It was hilarious. Even though I was at home, my feet started killing me by about 2.30 am, so the shoes were thrown into the cupboard under the stairs. My recent snog boy hadn't turned up, but to be honest, I wouldn't have noticed if he had. However, I would have noticed Patrick Swayze, especially if he had come in as Johny Castle and we had done 'The Lift'. I had had a brilliant night in the comfort of my own home. Grandad and some family members had left before midnight, and I understood. My Dad walked my Grandad down to his house at number 10. I secretly opened my card from Grandad. As I opened a cheque for £50, it fell out accompanied by an amazing message written on the birthday card in his beautiful handwriting.

Happy 18th birthday to my elegant granddaughter. Obviously, not with it, I thought. It continued briefly, *here's some money for your next few Pina Coladas. Love Grandad.* This brought a tear to my eye. He was a proud and strict man, but he had a soft side. I opened this card on the sly and put the cheque in my Dad's bureau in the front room for safety.

By 3.00 am, it was just me and my Labellos friends sitting in the conservatory drinking, smoking and talking well, gossiping about people who came into the bar and laughing about various scenarios we had witnessed on our shifts. Mum and Dad had gone to bed by now, giving me a look as if to say, 'Don't be up all night'.

The Silk Cut cigarettes were in full flow, and I am sure I'd emptied the ashtrays at least a hundred times tonight. Soul II Soul was playing in the background as we put the world to the right and ended up telling each other secrets that only came out after copious amounts of alcohol.

I looked to my left, and Sharon was unconscious on one of the rattan sofas with one of the dogs' blankets over her. To my right were my work friends. I would never have thought I would get so close to people after a few months of working together.
I worried about being sick when I was going for the first interview and panicking over my black pants. Looking back, I had nothing to worry about, and my life would start getting exciting now.

Chapter 7

"MUM" WHERE'S MY black pants? You know the good ones? I need them for work. She's probably washed them on a hot wash, and they will only fit a small child now, or even worse, have creases ironed down the front. I remember she did that once when I was a child. I had a pair of jeans with Scooby Doo characters down the front. Well, they were characters until she ironed the faces of Fred and Daphne.

I worked as a glass collector in one of the trendiest bars in Liverpool's city centre. It was quite a novelty this place. There were mostly Irish-themed or old-man pubs that stunk of cigarettes and stale beer. I could not wait until I was 18 because I could start serving drinks. I used to have a babysitting job for some rich couple who lived by mine. I noticed an advert in the Post Office window at the top of my road asking for a babysitter 2 nights a week. I rang up in my poshest voice and went to see them the day after. They lived about 10 minutes from me in a massive house, all singing and dancing with CD players in every room and big posh draped curtains with swags and tails. Quite tacky, to be honest. And loads of cushions everywhere!

I started babysitting the next day, and the kids were little shits. Spoilt rotten! But it was easy money. £10. That would easily pay for a night out. I could have been a lunatic, but they didn't care; they just wanted someone asap so they could go out on the town. I would get there at about 7.00 and get home at about 12. I used to ring all my mates most of the night because the phone at home had a lock on it. I had learnt how to tap it as long as there wasn't a 0 in the number!

I did this job for a few months, but the money was nowhere near enough, so I started looking through the pages of the Thursday Night Echo. Job night. I didn't have any idea what I was looking for, but the advert made me look twice. I wasn't going to apply, but then I thought, sod, it was worth a try.

The bar in question was called Labellos. The advert asked for dynamic people who wanted to work in the Newest Bar in the Northwest. Obviously, that was me. Well, it was in the end. I applied for the job and was contacted a few weeks later to go for an interview. Honestly, I'd forgotten I'd even applied for it. My mum drove me there and waited for me afterwards; I hadn't had any interviews before but thought I'd hope for the best. "Just be yourself, my love," Mum said a dozen times. I was nervous enough, and this pep talk was making me worse.

"I will, Mum," and I gave her a look as if to say shut up now.

It went well, and it must have been because they rang me the next day to ask me to go for a second interview. For god's sake, it was only a bar job, not working for MI5!

I went to the second interview on my own this time; I couldn't be bothered with Mum's words of wisdom on this occasion. They told me I had been successful in my application. I was made up; I didn't even know what job I had got. They said training would start in a week and would last 5 days. This must be someplace I thought to have training, but I had no idea what I would do as I only ever had a babysitting job.

The Wonder Bra Years

A week later I arrived at the bar on London Street in the city centre. I was a confident 17-year-old, but when I arrived, this confidence was slightly knocked out of me.

About 7 other girls were there; most looked glamorous and older than me. I turned up in jeans and a black T-shirt and borrowed one of my mum's jackets with shoulder pads. I would wear my denim jacket, but I thought I'd decided to make an effort. I also put a necklace on with pearls and fake diamonds, trying to look sophisticated. The other girls on the training course were so pretty. As I walked into the room, I went quiet momentarily, and they looked me up and down. "Hi, I'm Nicky," I announced as confident as I could. They all introduced themselves individually. Almost immediately forgot every name.

The training consisted of health and safety, customer service, etc. I quickly made friends with some other girls, and two fellas thought they were god's gift. Even though I was only going to be the glass collector until I turned 18, I still had to learn all the basics. A couple of them were quite standoffish; they loved themselves. Definitely not my type of person, but I faked being nice as best as I could just so I would fit in.

Labellos was the first of its kind. I mean, I obviously didn't know much about bars and pubs, but it certainly looked the part. The interior was based on a French wine bar with authentic beer pumps and wine served by glass and bottle, along with some outrageous cocktails called Sex on the Beach and Multiple Orgasm. The shame of asking for one of these!!

We were told the uniform would be black trousers (I had hundreds of pairs), a white shirt and a waistcoat with a man's tie. When I went home, I asked my dad for a tie, and he gave me a choice of a paisley print or one with flowers. I thought either was cool enough, so I went to Burton the next day and bought a cool stripey one in the sale. While shopping, I treated myself to a new top by Chelsea Girl and a pair of stilettos by Dolcis. In the sale, I was thrilled. Always after a bargain, I was.

At the end of the training, the managers took all the staff for a meal in a Mexican restaurant in the city centre. I had never eaten food like this. I was only used to going to The Bernie Inn or Wimpy. The food in the restaurant was all salsa, guacamole and sour cream, and it looked disgusting and very wet. I pretended to enjoy it as I did not want to appear immature in front of my new work friends. I placed most of my meal into my serviette when no one was looking. They all decided to go out for drinks after the meal, but I didn't go as I didn't feel like I fit in at this point, and I wanted to get the last bus home. They were all talking about boys, snogging and sex, and it made me feel uncomfortable even though I was not a wallflower by any means, more like a dandelion or a weed. Little did I know how much my life would change the following year.

Chapter 8

SHARON AND I had been friends for a few years. I met her through a mutual friend who lived by me. When my friend introduced me to Sharon, we hit it off immediately. We had the same warped sense of humour, liked the same music and liked to go to the same pubs in town on the few occasions we had managed to sneak out.

The first time I went to a nightclub I was only 15. A girl in the year above me in school was having a supposed 18th birthday night out in a club called Gino's. Every Friday, this club would always advertise in the Echo that the party organiser got a free bottle of bubbly for organising a party. More like Cresta lemonade than bubbly!! I wouldn't say I was forced to go to this 18th, but I felt I had to so I wouldn't feel left out.

"Shall we go?" Sharon enquired. "It will be a laugh; we can get drunk on the way there; we might cop off."

I thought about it for a few seconds and said yes to her proposal. "Your mum won't let you," I replied. Sharon's mum was a lot stricter than mine.

I've always had a very open and honest relationship with my mum. She was cool, to be honest, not like other strict mums. But I knew she would trust me more if I told her the truth. I told her about this party, and she wasn't too sure at first as I was only 15, after all.

"Nicky, the town is full of drunks and perverts only after one thing; I'll have to think about this"

Eventually, she agreed with certain conditions. Do not drink spirits, and be home around 12. 12? Bloody hell, but rules were rules.

So, the night-out planning started about 4 weeks before. The first thing was getting hold of some ID. My friend's sister had a provisional driving license that made her 18, so I had to practice my false name and date of birth! The second thing was what to wear.

I had a look through my mum's wardrobe for suitable items that would make me look older but not like something from Dallas or Dynasty. I found a black jacket with sequins on it, shoulder pads that looked okay, and a black mini-skirt that was quite tight-fitted. All I needed now was a top. I could steal a pair of my mum's tights, too, but definitely not the American tan ones. Dot Cotton springs to mind with these.

Sharon and I got together a few times beforehand to practice our hair and makeup. I already had plenty of Insette hairspray and Rimmel's usual azure blue mascara and sugar plum pink lipstick. I robbed (borrowed without permission, I think) my mum's Arabian glow bronzer along with her Leichner foundation, which was as thick as mud!

I decided to start looking for a top in my mum's Grattan catalogue. She also had Littlewoods and Marshall Ward. She didn't buy much from there, but occasionally, we would get things if we needed them for a special occasion.

I saw a few tops that I liked. One was a black and white polka dot boob tube and the other was a cerise pink fitted top with

The Wonder Bra Years

frills on. I decided to order both. I already had an elasticated Waspie belt and high heels, so I was nearly there. The boob tube top would need a padded bra though.

A few days later, the white arrow van pulled up outside my house.

"Have you been ordering from the catalogue?" Mum's voice bellowed up the stairs.

"Yes, Mum, sorry, it's only £1.00 a week" (for the rest of my teenage years!). I could tell she was furious. I waited till she went out to the shops before I went downstairs.

When the coast was clear, I made my way downstairs. I opened the package and tried both tops on with the black mini skirt. I decided to keep both. One for the night out, one for a treat, and hopefully another night out. Eventually, the day arrived. I woke up feeling half excited and half feeling like I was going to throw up. Sharon and I had decided to start getting ready about 2pm even though we weren't meeting everyone till 7pm!!! Well, a girl had to try and make an effort, didn't she?

Sharon arrived at about 2.45. She was always late, but I was always one to be on time for anything. She had brought practically a black bin bag to mine with about six different outfit combinations. We spent an hour or so trying on different outfits.

"What about this top with the cerise pink skirt." Sharon did a twirl.

"I prefer the black skirt with the Jade green top," I replied. Sharon looked at herself in the full-length mirror again and did another outfit change. Tenth of the day, I think.

She eventually decided on black trousers with an electric blue top and a black Waspie belt. I had decided on the polka dot boob tube with my mum's skirt and tights with a padded Wonderbra under as I was very conscious of the size of my boobs. Well, basically, I didn't have any. Well, not compared to my friends. I was so jealous.

We were ready at 5.30, so we had a sneaky glass of martini I had stolen from my mum and dad's booze cabinet. There wasn't any lemonade so we had to have Dandelion and Burdock with it. It was disgusting, but after one glass, I felt a bit warm and fuzzy, so it had served its purpose.

We went downstairs, and the noise of our high heels on the stairs alerted my mum, so she joined us in the hall. She looked us up and down. "For god's sake, Nicky! Have you got enough makeup?" said my mum in an annoyed tone as she looked at my drag queen-esque face. I thought I'd done it okay, I thought to myself! "And what's that bloody smell?" The smell was Poison perfume, which we were both currently wearing. It was a fake version, so it probably smelt more like cat piss than perfume. My mum had decided she was going to pick me up at midnight just to make sure I got home on time because it was my first time on a big night out. "I'll be outside just before midnight, girls. Don't have me waiting, please." "We won't we said in unison."

We left the house and started walking and giggling to ourselves on the way to the bus stop. We could not believe we were actually out.

"Promise you won't leave me, Nic" I stopped walking and grabbed Sharon's arms. "Behave we must stay together at all times, promise?" "Promise," she nodded.

I had a black clutch bag with my money, lipstick, fake ID and some tissues. I didn't need a hairbrush because my hair was backcombed so much and rock solid from the hairspray. We were meeting everyone outside the club at 6.45pm. The club opened at 7pm, so we wanted to make sure we definitely got in. I started panicking about getting knocked back by the bouncers and started practising my fake name and date of birth again. I even got Sharon to test me on the way there. We got on the 85 bus, and it would take about 30 minutes. Before getting on the bus, we went to the off-license and bought a bottle of cider. We sat upstairs at the back of the bus so no one would see us and tell the driver.

The cider was quite strong, and Sharon was getting louder and louder. We were passing the bottle to each other, having a good swig. "Shush, will you? You'll get us thrown off." She just giggled. "I love you, Nicky; you're the best friend ever; promise we will be friends forever and ever." "I promised, reached over to her, and gave her the warmest hug I think I had ever given anyone. I felt a bit woozy, but the more we drank, the more money we would save in the club. We also had a cigarette on the bus. Ten silk cut between us. We had half each. That made me feel really dizzy, and I felt like I was going to get sick. I had smoked before, mainly because of peer pressure, but I thought smoking would make me look older. Sharon had some polo mints, so I grabbed a few of her to make me feel better.

We got into town at 6.30, so we sat on a bench near the club for 15 minutes, had another cigarette between us and had a final practice of our dates of birth.

At 6.45, we walked up to the entrance of Gino's. It was lit up with blue neon lights, and the name Gino's was bright pink neon above the door. We saw a few of our friends who were there already and screamed when we saw each other all dressed up. The scrutinisation of our outfits started with mostly everyone saying, "Oh, you look gorgeous, love." I'm such an awful liar.

7pm came and went, and the club didn't open. We were all freezing by now and couldn't wait to get in the warm. Eventually, at 7.15, we heard the unlocking of a door, and an older man opened two big, thick wooden doors and held them open with stools. Next to him were two big bouncers in black suits and dickie bows. They signalled the front of the queue to start making their way inside. My heart sank; what if I didn't get in? What if I trip in my high heels? I was truly worrying about anything and everything that could happen. We were about four people behind the entrance, and the bouncers asked for the sight of ID and the party invitation that gave us free admission.

"Right you," as I grabbed Sharon's wrist. "Head high, and don't make eye contact with the bouncers."

'But! What?" She mumbled.

"But, what, nothing? "I replied. "Act cool." The entrance queue was moving quickly.

It was my turn next, and Sharon followed. I walked up, and the larger of the two bouncers looked me up and down. He then gave me a cheeky smile and said, "Go on, love" show your ticket to the girl at the desk.

I'd done it; I was in. And so was Sharon.

Chapter 9

GINO'S WAS UNREAL. As we walked in, I could hear Never Too Much by Luther Vandross! The entrance was very dark and dingy but the club was wow! The dancefloor was lit up with flashing lights, and around the outside were tall tables with high-back silver chairs with a plush velvet seat and neon lights almost everywhere. I giggled as the white part of my top lit up in the neon. As you walked around the dancefloor towards the back of the club, there were more tables and chairs and then the bar. Sharon, a few of the other girls, and I made our way to a group of tables where our party had set up camp.

"Nicky, Nicky, can you believe it!" Sharon's face was a picture.

"No, I can't," I laughed, "but don't let your defences down; we need to get served at the bar yet." All that worrying for nothing. Good job, really, as I'd totally forgotten my fake date of birth already.

Lorraine, whose supposed 18th it was, was all giddy and excited as a glamorous blond-haired woman came over with a bigger-than-normal bottle of fizz and six glasses. It was like feeding time at the zoo, with everyone clambering for a free drink in a champagne flute. I managed to get half a glass that I knocked back in one (Dutch courage, I've been told you call it). We were the only ones in the club currently; after all, it was only 7.30. I went up to the bar as confidently as I could and ordered two halves of cider and blackcurrant. It was happy hour until

9pm, and buy one get one free, so I was bloody delighted. £1.25 for two halves!

Result, we got served without any trouble. We took our drinks back to the tables we had accommodated and sat down so we could sit back for a moment and get over the fact that we had got into a nightclub with no trouble at all. All that worry for nothing. We had worked out our money so we could get four more ciders each before the end of the happy hour.

Gino's was a bit of a cheesy nightclub, not that I was an expert or anything. Chart music and pop. As we were drinking our drinks, we heard loads of songs that we loved that had been in the Top Ten, or I had heard my Mum play. When I was a kid, I used to ask my Mum to put her Abba record on for me in the front room, and I would dance to all the songs. Every now and again, my big feet would make a song skip, and my Mum would come in and tell me off just in case I scratched the vinyl with my elephant feet. I always had big feet and really long toes. I hated it when the foot nurse used to come into school. I used to hide my feet under the wooden PE bench, so I wouldn't get skitted by my classmates. However, having big feet had its advantages when the sales were on in Dolcis and Ravel, as the size 7's would always be left and reduced the most.

An hour or so passed and Gino's was filling up. To the left of us, there was a table of older women who seemed to be also celebrating a birthday, and to the right, a gang of lads that seemed to be eyeing up a few in our party. Think they were on a stag night because one of the lads was dressed up in a

Hawaiian shirt and a pair of small swimming trunks. I didn't mean to look at it, but I was curious, and some of it was poking out the sides. We also made sure we stocked up on our drinks before 9pm. This probably wasn't a good idea.

Lorraine, whose party it was, seemed very experienced in flirting with the opposite sex. I was fascinated by her and was practically watching her every move. The way she flicked her hair and the way she walked. I couldn't flick my hair as it was rock solid; an earthquake would not move mine. One of her friends, Chantelle, came over to us to see how we were. She was one of the cool girls in school. "Have you two been out before?" She enquired while chewing gum and blowing bubbles. "Err yeh loads of times," I answered. I did not know what to say, and I definitely didn't want to look like a baby.

"Really, like where? Have you been to The Hippodrome?"

"Yeh, loads of times," I answered. "Didn't really like it, full of poseurs." I saw Sharon's jaw drop, and I gave her a sly nudge with my elbow as if to signal for backup.

"Yeh," she piped up. "Not really our scene, is it, Nic?" she said as she picked up her glass and slurped a big slurp of her cider. Chantelle seemed impressed by our response and signalled to Lorraine to send us another glass of fake champagne. "Enjoy, girls," she said as she turned her back and went back to her table. Sharon and I looked at each other and the two new champagne flutes in front of us and burst into hysterics. We were having such an amazing night; it really was brilliant.

We drank our newly acquired drink and continued to watch Lorraine flirt her way through every possible boy in the vicinity. It truly was amazing what she did. She had somehow ended up sitting with these men at their table, and then she ended up on someone's knee! I found myself staring in awe as I watched Lorraine flirt her way to free drinks and eventually necking one of the fellas. I remember not knowing what necking was when I first heard the phrase. I thought it was rubbing your neck with someone else's neck. Thank God I never had the chance to try out my theory.

After I came out of my trance watching Lorraine, I turned to my side to nudge Sharon, but she was nowhere to be seen. "Where's Sharon" I turned to the girl opposite me. She shrugged her shoulders, so I got up from my seat to find her. I remembered our promise to each other on the bus.

I walked towards the bar, no sign! I looked at the dancefloor, which had filled up a bit by the time with the sound of Rick James Superfreak. I then made my way towards the toilets. Surely she must be here, and low and behold, I was greeted by the sound of someone wrenching their guts out in the far cubicle.

"Sharon, is that you?" I shouted from outside the cubicle.

"Eerghh, yes," I heard her voice.

"Open the door," I demanded, worried sick about her.

The door unlocked, and Sharon had her head next to the toilet seat, and the bowl was full of purple liquid. I pissed myself laughing! What a waste of cider and black times ten.

"Nicky, I feel awful," she groaned.

"Wait here," I said, "I'll go and get you some water." I went to the bar and asked for a glass of water. The barmaid looked at me funny; they probably hadn't served any water all evening.

I took the half pint of lukewarm water into the toilet and walked up to the end cubicle to Sharon, who by this time seemed to have recovered slightly, as she was now sitting up, and she started laughing as soon as she saw me.

"Drink this," I said as I passed the lukewarm glass of tap water. Sharon took the glass and proceeded to swig in one.

"Ew, it's warm," she moaned. I gave her an annoyed look! "Get it down, you and shut up," I giggled. "Come on, we've only got an hour and a half left." Sharon eventually stood up and made her way to the sink to wash her hands and reapply her lipstick.

"I feel like a new woman now, Nic," as she grabbed my hand. Her hand was wet, and I just hoped it was water and not puke.

Mum was coming at 12.00, so I wanted to make the most of my first time in the adult world of nightclubbing. And I also didn't want to annoy Mum.

We went back into the club, and by this time, 11pm, it was busy. There were groups of men and women everywhere, with the odd splattering of couples who were looking romantic and kissing every now and again. To be honest, I felt embarrassed for them; I could not imagine doing that in public! The shame.

We heard Wham I'm Your Man playing, so we danced our way to the dancefloor. We had a right laugh and were having the

The Wonder Bra Years

time of our lives. The balls of my feet were killing me by now, and I noticed a ladder in my tights. Great!

However, I felt like Cinderella waiting for the stroke of midnight. I looked at my watch constantly. I even annoyed myself at one point, but I was so conscious of not being late. I loved my swatch watch; it was a clear strap swatch watch I had got for Christmas last year. I'm sure it was a limited edition one. Anyway, we had 15 minutes left.

We swigged our drinks in one and made our way onto the bustling dancefloor for one last dance. Word Up by Cameo was playing; I loved this song. We then said our goodbyes to our friends. Some of them said bye, and some started laughing at us for leaving so early. I was a bit miffed and embarrassed to be leaving as early as this, but all I could think of was how lucky I was to be here and not like some of my friends who had been forbidden from attending. I looked for Lorraine to say thank you for inviting me, but she was playing tonsil tennis with another boy and not the one whose knee she was sitting on, so she was not to be interrupted. I definitely needed some tips from her, so I left her to it. I also noticed the stag on the way out slumped in a corner with a missing Hawaiian shirt. At least his pants were still intact; it's a shame other bits were not!

We walked outside at 12.05 am, and Mum was standing outside with our dog Sally, who barked as soon as she saw me. She jumped up at me and pulled a ladder in my tights, well, my Mum's tights. Oh well, I was only going home. Mum started to give me the Spanish Inquisition in the car on the way home.

"Well, what was it like? What did you drink? Was anyone sick." I glanced over at Sharon, who had her head in her hands; I was not going to get any sense out of her.   "It was great, Mum," I started. "The music was brilliant; loads of songs that you play at home." I was trying to suck up to her so that she wouldn't twig on that Sharon was almost certainly about to be sick again. Mum started babbling about going out in her day, and it was so much better than today, blah blah. I looked over at Sharon, and I could tell that she was about to explode.

"Mum, stop the car, please. I think Sharon is going to be sick." Mum glanced back and pulled over as soon as it was safe. I opened the door next to Sharon, and immediately, she pebble-dashed the pavement and the side of Mum's Nissan Micra. It was pandemonium as Sally tried to get out of the car, thinking she was at the park for wee-wees. We managed to restrain her until Sharon managed to sit upright again next to me in the back seat.

"Wow, I feel so much better now; sorry about that." I could tell my Mum was fuming as she started the engine again. I gave Sharon a stern glare. For God's sake, how much can one person be sick?

We dropped Sharon off outside her house, made sure she got inside safely and then went home. "What the bloody hell have you been drinking, Nicky? You need to be more careful; she could have choked on her own vomit." I had a quick think of what to say, I never lied to Mum, but in this instance, I decided to.

"Mum, we had two halves of cider, I promise, I think Sharon was spiked or something." God strike me down for lying, but it was only a white lie wasn't it? As soon as I got in, a wave of exhaustion hit me, and I fell into bed. I didn't even wash my face or clean my teeth. As I lay in bed, my ears were ringing, and the balls of my feet were throbbing. What a night!!

Chapter 10

MY HEAD WAS banging when I woke up! My mouth was dry, and I was dying for water. I got up and filled a mug with water from the bathroom tap; I didn't care if it tasted bad; I just swigged it like someone stranded in the desert. I then realised the mug by my bed had been there for almost a week; I decided to ignore the green mould floating at the top. My face was still full of last night's makeup, and I stunk of booze and stale perfume. I felt dreadful. I started running a bath, hoping that my Dad had put the hot water on earlier. Lucky for me, he had.

My Mum was hoovering downstairs, and my Dad was pottering in the garden. I'm sure my Mum was doing this on purpose to wake me up banging into every possible skirting board. We had a lovely garden, and my Dad was like Percy Thrower. I thought it was the most boring thing ever, but he loved it. Every time my Auntie came around, she and my Dad would end up in the garden talking about plants and flowers. My Auntie even knew the Latin name of most of the shrubs.

I fell into my nice, warm bath. I almost fell asleep at one point because I was shattered.

It was Saturday lunchtime and usually on a Saturday we went shopping in town even if we had no money, all we needed was our bus fare. This week, however, I had no choice but to stay in after I had spoken to Sharon, and I found out she was grounded as she had been sick again when she got home, and her Mum hit the roof.

"Nicky, it was all up the bathroom door and on my Mum's new white slippers, pure dark purple." I could not help laughing, but Sharon's Mum was really angry, mainly worried as he could have choked on her own vomit! Is this just a saying old people say, I thought?

Weirdly Sharon felt perfectly fine today, and it was me that felt like shit. Probably puked all hers out. Even worse, her Mum had just decorated the bathroom. Purple rinse on the newly painted white doors. Oops.

On a usual weekend, Sharon would get the bus or walk to the top of my road, where I would meet her, and we would get the bus into town. We would get off at Lewis's Department Store and have a wander through there. Usually, the makeup department, to try and to get some free samples, and occasionally the clothes department, but they were a bit expensive in there for our budget.

We would then make our way to St John's Market. It wasn't a proper market. It was indoors with various stalls, but I hated it in that part of our Saturday afternoons because the smell of fish from the Fishmonger stall was vile. Sharon used to wind me up because she loved crabsticks and always wanted to buy some, so she stunk afterwards.

A few of the clothes stalls were ok. They had versions of clothes that were sold in High Street stores but a bit cheaper. I really wanted a Dash tracksuit, but they were far too expensive, so one day, I ended up buying a similar version in a baby blue colour. It was only £15, so it would probably fall apart after two washes! I made a note to myself, don't let my Mum near it.

I didn't want to spend any money today anyway because I wanted to save my money for the next night out even though it had not even been arranged or suggested yet. I was babysitting tonight, too, so that was another ten pounds going out of my funds. I dozed on and off most of the day, and then I had my tea, crispy pancakes, chips and beans - a proper kids' tea. Sharon sometimes came to babysit with me, but I think tonight was a no-no. I didn't want to call her either; I was too scared of what her Mum would say to me.

I cleaned myself up, made myself half presentable, and left my house around 6.45pm. I had to be at Yvonne's house at 7pm. Her husband worked in finance in some shape or form, so he was in London all week and came home at weekends. I babysat Tuesdays and Saturdays. Yvonne went out with her friends on a Tuesday while her husband, Mark, was away. She used to pay me £15 or £20 on a Tuesday if I agreed to sleep over. Basically, she could stay out late or all night, as sometimes happened. Hush money, definitely. I didn't mind, to be honest, apart from her kids that I hated and a Bichon Frisé dog that always had a poo in the bed I was meant to be sleeping in. Dirty little shit.

Yvonne's husband, Mark, was a bit of a perv; I always felt uneasy around him. Yvonne was very glamorous. She was slim, with big boobs, long blond hair and she had amazing clothes. Everything I wanted. I really liked her, and I didn't think she suited Mark, so I guessed she married him for the money and lifestyle because it definitely wasn't his personality or his looks.

As soon as I arrived at the house, they were ready to leave. She always got me nice food from Marks and Spencer, and I was starving, so all was good. I definitely made the most of it. We never had food like this in our house. I remember tasting houmous for the first time and I was pleasantly surprised even though it looked like cat sick.

They had 3 children. The two younger ones were lovely, but the elder one was a little shit. Always bossing the little ones around and trying to cause trouble. It was late on that I found out he had a different dad, so that was probably why he acted up. Attention-seeking shit.

"I want a sandwich now," the little shit cried right into my face. I wanted to give him a bunch of fives but decided against child abuse for this evening. Instead, I smiled and made my way to the fridge. So I decided to put a bit of Tabasco sauce in his lovely jam sandwich. Serves him right! He was crying and gasping for water after a minute or so. I denied all knowledge. I just said the jam must have been on the turn.

Mark and Yvonne would get home not long after midnight on the weekend, and he would sometimes offer to drive me home. He had a flash Jaguar car, and it was not till later that I realised he was definitely drunk driving. I didn't live far away, but the roads were very dark where they lived as it was on the outskirts of a park. One time, he put his hand on my knee, squeezed it and gave me a look. You know that type of look! "I can take you the long way home if you want" he smiled as he spoke. It made me feel sick. Dirty bastard. I politely declined. After that happened, I never accepted a lift home from him again, and I was thinking twice about even doing any more babysitting. Luckily, the Labellos job was on the horizon, and I didn't have to see him again.

The next day was Sunday. I had a lie-in and then went to the corner shop to get the Sunday papers. I loved reading all the celebrity gossip, who was sleeping with whom, etc.

My Grandad came for Sunday lunch every fortnight. He lived on the same road as us, and as my Nan had passed away a few years earlier, we wanted to look after him as much as he would allow. We were a close family but not the type that lived in each other's pockets.

Lunch would be served in the conservatory at the back of the house and it was either freezing in the winter or absolutely boiling whenever a bit of sun came out. My Mum always made a fabulous lunch and served it in her Hostess trolley; she definitely had her money's worth of that thing; it was her pride and joy. After lunch, we would all sit in the front room, a room that was hardly used for special occasions or when I wanted to dance to Abba as a child. My Grandad was obsessed with golf, so we always had to watch it if it was on, and often it was. I still know what a birdie or an eagle is now! Nick Faldo was his favourite.

Grandad would leave around 5pm, and we watched him walk up the road from our doorstep in case he fell. He was a tall, well-mannered man. Ex-police, so he was very straight in every way possible. He never showed any emotion or love. You just knew he cared.

Early night then for me. I had sixth form in the morning. I was doing GCSE re-sits. I passed a few but wanted higher grades and couldn't be bothered having a full-time job with responsibility yet, but I definitely needed more money.

At the end of the term, I ended up getting the job in Labellos and started working there because the money for someone of my age was too good to be true. All of a sudden, I grew up in more ways than one. And I didn't go back to babysitting after that incident. Oh, and I didn't pass my re-sits either, so it was a good thing I had a job to go to.

Chapter 11

I WORKED VARIOUS shifts in the bar. It was open from midday till 11pm most days. I worked in the kitchen, helping prepare food during the day and then some evenings as a glass collector. I was originally taken on as part-time, but seeing as I failed my initial exams and re-sits, I started to ask for extra shifts. After a few weeks, I was doing 40-odd hours a week as it was really busy.

I didn't have any official catering training, but I did learn a lot about cooking and preparing food. The food that was on the menu was not your usual pub food. They did ribs, nachos, chicken wings with dips, all fancy. Not a bit like the Bernie Inn. I didn't really want to work in the kitchen but was too young to work behind the bar. However, I was promised some bar shifts as soon as I turned 18. I started working the odd evening as a glass collector. This started one weekend when a few of the staff called in sick, so I offered to help as I was dying to work upstairs.

"Nicky, you free tonight? I need someone to collect glasses" The Manager didn't have to ask me twice. This was my chance to get upstairs and feel the thrill of the bar at its best. I got ready asap with a bit more make-up than usual ready for my shift; I couldn't wait.

I felt special and a part of a cool group. The people who came to the bar were all really trendy and seemed to have plenty of money. Probably all an act, but it was certainly convincing to me. Also, a few famous faces would pop in, especially on Saturday nights. Footballers from the local teams would always be there with loads of girls flocking around them. I ended up friends with some of them because I didn't hassle them. On one occasion, a certain footballer behaved inappropriately toward a girl in the back part of the bar!! I could not wait to get the Sunday Paper the next day to see if it was mentioned. And it was.

I made loads of friends working in Labellos and started to have an amazing social life. As the staff of a very popular venue, we were always invited to the VIP openings of new bars in the city centre, usually on a Thursday, and they always had free drinks. It was on one of these nights I made a pig of myself on the free booze and was that sick. I'm sure Bacardi was coming out of my nose at one point!! Put me off it for life. Well, for at least a few months.

We used to have a laugh too. One day, a kitchen porter started working in the kitchen. He was only young and a bit of a scally but a nice enough lad. We had a sort of initiation ceremony that we would do for all new staff. This day, the head chef asked the young lad to go to the Italian restaurant opposite to ask to borrow a certain ingredient.

"Lad, just go to the Italian for me please and ask him if he's got any spare cunnilingus sauce." The chef and his assistant were crying and laughing as this poor lad walked over to the restaurant over the road. I pretended to understand the joke, but I didn't have a clue. Five minutes later, I knew what it was. I remember someone telling me once that they asked the new YTS boy on a painting and decorating course to go to Rapid Hardware and get some Tartan paint and some bubbles for a spirit level.

We cried laughing when he came back and called us all the bastards under the sun. So funny. Luckily, I didn't have any pranks played on me because I was one of the original staff members, so the ritual wasn't in place then. In fact, I was probably the main instigator.

Eventually, I turned 18 and was promoted to bar staff. It felt amazing, the atmosphere was so good upstairs in the bar area and the tips were amazing. One customer we nicknamed Mr Budweiser as he always had this beer and gave fifty pence a tip every time, and that soon mounted up. Certain regulars were renowned for tipping, so every member of staff would always want to serve them first as a tip was guaranteed. "Take your own love" became a saying I would hear numerous times a day. 20p was the expected amount unless they were absolutely paralytic, and the odd £1.00 was taken. My first Christmas working behind the bar was fantastic. By 1 pm Christmas Eve, the bar was full, and one time, I made over £80 in tips alone because everyone was in such a generous Christmassy mood. If I had heard Slade one more time one particular time, I would have actually started a petition so that it could only be played twice in a twelve-hour period. I decided against this as I assumed John Major had more important things to discuss in parliament.

My fashion sense also changed dramatically at this time. Before starting to work here, I wasn't at all bothered or interested, but as I watched all the people come and go in the bar, I was obsessed with what they were wearing. A lot of the shops in the area were either stockists of designer clothes or alternative fashion that was interesting but not too wacky. A shop called Drome opened close by, and it stocked Vivienne Westwood and John Richmond clothes, amongst other designer names. I loved them all. I saved up for the latest tops and dresses that you couldn't get on the high street. I wasn't an attention seeker, but I liked to look good.

For someone of my age, I was earning good money. If I added my tips to my wages, I was earning about £150 plus a week, and that was on a bad week. I gave my Mum £10 a week and spent the rest on clothes and going out.

A few months later, Sharon and I decided to book a holiday.

"Sharon, we need a holiday, sun, sea and maybe sex" I giggled and blushed at the same time as I brought up my suggestion. She was well up for it. I was earning quite good money now, but Sharon was always skint. It was always me buying the fags and the cider. However, luckily, her Nan had died a few months before and left her some money, so for once, she actually had some money, and she was well up for it.

"Well, it's what Nana Norma would have wanted to see her granddaughter enjoy her life with the money she had left her" Sharon dictated to me in a sincere ish voice.

"As long as Nana Norma doesn't see you having sex with anyone, that is," I replied as we both cried, laughing and hugged each other and jumped up and down with excitement for the anticipation of our first girl's holiday.

We went to Lunn Poly in Town the following weekend and sat with the travel agent and we told her what we wanted. To be honest, we didn't really know what we wanted apart from the obvious Sun, Sea, etc. We had picked up a few brochures a few weeks before, but we had no clue; we knew we did not want to end up in the back of beyond.

The travel agent found us two weeks in Crete for £250 self-catering going in July. It was a self-catering apartment in the busy resort in Malia. We bit her hand off and paid the total balance there and then, as it was only 2 months till we flew out, and we couldn't wait.

The holiday planning started almost immediately. The first thing was starting a diet. I was a size 10-12 with no shape, but the thought of being in a bikini in front of loads of people filled me with fear. Sharon was a bit bigger than me, and she had great boobs, but I always told her she looked great. I hated my boobs; they were so small compared to the Pamela Anderson ones that every man wanted a girl to have. We both went to Boots one Saturday and bought some slim fast. Strawberry flavour should be consumed as a drink instead of as a meal. I think I lasted one day; I liked my food too much. We were going for two weeks, so that meant I needed at least 14 different outfits for the nighttime. How the hell was I going to afford that?

"Nic, we will have to get some stuff from the catalogue; we can mix and match." I looked at Sharon in disbelief.

"Are you mad, I replied, "We still owe my mum for the other clothes from last year." Anyway, we had a look, and we ordered a couple of sarongs that we could share and a pair of jelly shoes for each. Sharon got a lovely petite pair in pink in a size 5 and I got a dinosaur size pair in Black. I also ordered an underwired padded bikini on the sly and just hoped my Mum wouldn't notice until we came home and I got some more wages to pay her.

Obviously, I had some things in my wardrobe already, but I needed more bikinis with padding and underwired, sarongs, shorts, t-shirts and dresses. It's always nice to have new stuff for your holiday, I thought to myself.

We went shopping a few weeks before. "Where are we starting Nic?" Sharon was so excited. She still had some money left from Nane Norma to buy some clothes and the rest would be spending money.

"Let's get off the Bus at Lewis's and make our way down Church Street."

We started in Kumar when we got off the bus, then made our way to Miss Selfridge, Chelsea Girl, Oasis and Top Shop. I got some shorts, a few T-shirts and vests from Miss Selfridge, and a bikini with the essential padding from Chelsea Girl. I ordered some other bits from my Auntie's Freemans catalogue, so I was pretty much sorted with the stuff I already had. I already had a lovely pair of sunglasses that I had treated myself to from an up-market shop by work. Emporio Armani tortoiseshell arms with gold frames. If I lose them, I will kill myself. Well, obviously, I won't, but I will be fuming!

My dad had got a suitcase out of the loft for me, and I started packing there. I bought bits and bobs of toiletries every week from Boots and started putting Sun-In on my hair to make it look blonder. I don't think it worked, to be honest, but I sprayed it on religiously anyway. My hair was a nightmare. As soon as there was an ounce of moisture in the air, the curls appeared. And they weren't even nice curls like Julia Roberts had in Pretty Woman. They were pathetic and awkward. Even hair straighteners didn't help. I was doomed. Note to self: take lots of hair bobbles and clamps! I started panicking about coming on my period on holiday. I worked out roughly that I should just finish my period the day we were going away. It better had cos I could not wear tampons, could never get them in. I always used press on towels, and they were so uncomfortable, so the thought of wearing one on holiday gave me the fear of God. You would see it through my bikini bottoms.

The holiday was booked with Club 18-30. They had a reputation for being wild or very sexually orientated. We only booked with them because it was £20 cheaper than with a more reputable company and the apartment was meant to be where all the action was. Sharon and I agreed there was no way we were going to get involved with all the stupid games they made you play! No way I'd die of shame.

"Nic, we are in no way doing the pathetic games they do" Sharon was really serious. I decided to wind her up.

"Oh, why not? It will be fun. I think we should book them all." The look I got was that type of look that would freeze water. I tried to keep a straight face, but I burst into laughter. "Piss off; no way are we subjecting ourselves to that shit." I was deadly serious and so was Sharon.

It was 7 days until D-Day, and I was so excited I could hardly sleep. I went to Lunn Poly to pick our tickets up and get our currency. £100 for the Drachma and £200 for traveller's cheques each, and we had some English money. All I had to do now was finish off my packing, and I was all set. Mum was taking us to the airport. Our flight from Manchester was at 5 am in the morning, so we had to get there at 3 am. Poor Mum, she must have been exhausted the next day, as we had been when we arrived in Crete. We had been awake for nearly 24 hours. However, my exhaustion soon disappeared when I got to the airport and my excitement took over.

Chapter 12

"BE CAREFUL, YOU two," Mum said as she gave a mean, over-the-top hug, "We will, I promise." And I did mean it. As streetwise as I thought I had become, being in a foreign country was still nerve-racking.

We walked to the check-in desk and, well, practically ran. I could barely carry my suitcase, my clothes, toiletries, hairdryer, and diffuser. My mum had packed bacon, cheese, tea, coffee, and a bag of sugar. It was when I was checking in I thought that the sugar might look like a bag of drugs! As we got to the front of the queue, I started worrying that my case might be over the weight allowance. When the check-in lady put it on the scales, I shut my eyes, but luckily, it was just at the limit; how, I'll never know. Wish I'd packed more now.

"Smoking or none smoking?" the check-in lady asked. "Smoking," I replied. Definitely need a fag, it's a four-hour flight!

Check-in gave us our check-in cards, and off we went through to duty-free. I was going to buy some perfume as my mum and dad had given me £30 in English money for the airport. As we walked through the airport, we noticed a few groups of lads who were drinking pints of lager and who seemed half-cut. One of them caught my eye, and I smiled; he smiled back with a wink! I hope he is on my flight and in my resort, I wish to myself. Probably not knowing my luck.

Duty-free was a maze of perfume, make-up, alcohol and cigarettes. I bought a bottle of Loulou as it was on offer and

The Wonder Bra Years

decided not to buy cigarettes as people had told me they were much cheaper in Greece. I already had 40 on me anyway.

We went through to the bar. It was only 4 am, but we decided to start our holiday off in the right way. "What do you want?" I asked Sharon.

"Erm Diet coke."

I looked into her eyes and grabbed her hand. "Listen to you. This is our first holiday together, hopefully, the first of many, and there is no way you have a bloody diet coke." So I ordered a Bacardi and Coke and a vodka and orange for Sharon. We got our drinks, paid a fortune and looked at each other. "Cheers, love," as I clinked my glass with hers. Bloody hell, it blew our heads off. I had my hand luggage with bits and bobs in it and my tape player. I'd made a few mix tapes at home so we could play them in the room and on the beach. As I looked around, I saw that most young people had the same idea. I'd taped most of the songs off the Top 40 the last few Sundays.

The lad I had noticed at check-in was seated not far from us with his mates. I caught him looking over a few times and smiling. He was gorgeous. "Have you seen them lads over there?" Sharon exclaimed.

"Which ones?" I said as I turned round coyly, knowing exactly who she meant. As I turned around, I caught his eye again, and he gave me a wink. "Oh, I hadn't noticed" Bloody right, I've noticed; I couldn't keep my eyes off him. In the nick of time, our flight number appeared on the board and told us to go to gate 5. This was our first flight together. We swigged our drinks off and picked up our bags. It wasn't my first time on a plane. I was lucky to go to Spain and Cyprus with my parents when I was younger, so I was familiar with the process, but I was still not an expert. This was Sharon's first holiday abroad, and I could tell she was getting nervous.

As we stood up, I noticed the gang of lads I had also stood up. Yes, I thought he was on my flight. He looked amazing. He had a Lacoste t-shirt on with a pair of jeans and nice crisp white Reebok trainers.

"The lads are on our flight," Sharon squealed in excitement.

"Oh, are they?" I answered as coolly as I could. What I really wanted to say was, Yes, I know he is. I mean, they are!

We made our way to the gate and stood in the queue to board the plane. Before long, we showed our boarding cards to the Air hostess and made our way to our seats. As they were smoking seats, they were at the back of the plane. Air 2000 was the airline, and it looked very posh. Sharon was so nervous as she had not flown before. I told her the usual stories about being safer to fly than be in a car, but I think it fell on deaf ears. We got to our seats, put our bags and cassette player in the overhead lockers, sat down, fastened our seatbelts, and started looking through the in-flight magazine and duty-free list.

Luckily, our flight was on time. The air hostesses came into the aisle and provided safety information for the passengers in case of disaster. Sharon's face was a picture, I was pissing myself laughing at her. I was dying for a ciggy, but you were not allowed to have one until the lights came on to take seatbelts off. The engines revved up, and we started moving. I grabbed Sharon's hand and squeezed it tightly. "This is it," I said we are off!

After about fifteen minutes, the seatbelt signs went off, and this also meant we could smoke. "You can undo your seatbelt now," I nudged Sharon.

"No way, I'm keeping this on." Sharon's face was a picture.

"How are you going to go for a wee?" I laughed. "You'll be okay in a minute when we get some drinks." She smiled and gave my hand a tight squeeze. The flight lasted four hours, so we had a couple of drinks before our meal. It wasn't even 7 am, but we had already had at least four shots of Bacardi and vodka! It was a breakfast-type meal in a foil tray with a fresh orange, and I had a coffee. I love plane food, but Sharon picked at hers; she's so fussy. I think it was nerves mainly that put her off eating. I went for a wee after my food and glanced up and down the plane, looking for him. I could not see him anywhere, even though I knew he was on this flight.

After that, I felt shattered, so I decided to try to sleep as we still had at least two hours to go before landing. I was freezing, so I had to ask for a blanket from the air hostess. It was like a dog blanket, but it did the job. I wrapped up and fell asleep. I woke up to the sound of an announcement by the captain. "Hello, everyone. I hope you have all had a good flight; we are starting to make our descent to Heraklion Airport. Just to let you know, you are arriving in fabulous weather, so I hope you enjoy your holiday and thank you for flying with Air 2000." I gave Sharon a nudge, and she woke up. "We are here," I whispered. She was well away. My mum had given me some barley sugar sweets to tide me over, as I always had sore ears. God love her. I quickly popped one into my mouth and gave Sharon one, forcing one into her mouth.

The landing was quite smooth. Sharon had her eyes closed the whole time. I could tell the noise of the engines, and the plane wheels made her feel extra anxious.

"It's fine." It's just the wheels." I was as reassuring as possible, but I was too busy looking out of the window at the beautiful blue sea and sandy beaches. All sorts of scenarios started going through my mind, and I hoped they might happen in the next two weeks.

The usual hustle and bustle of people getting their bags out of the overhead storage proceeded, but I just sat there and waited for the rush to die down. "You can take your seatbelt off now," I smirked as I undid Sharon's belt, and she opened her eyes and gave me a nervous smile. Then, the lad from the airport walked past our seats on his way off the plane and gave me another smile. I smiled back, and I felt a funny feeling that I was going to see him again.

As I stood by the door of the plane, the heat hit me and the smell of abroad. It was the best feeling ever. We made our way down the steps onto the runway, where a bus was waiting for us. We got on, and by this time, there were no seats, so we stood up, holding onto a canvas strap hanging from the ceiling. The bus started moving and jolted me forward right into the back of some man. "Sorry," I said just as Fitty turned round. Oh my god, it's him. I nicknamed him Fitty because he was so fit; he was just my type.

"It's okay," he said in a different accent than I was used to. I felt all flustered, and I was sure my face was bright red. "Hello, where are you staying?" He asked. "Malia, Georgios apartments."

"We are going to Malia," he replied, but not sure where. "Maybe we could meet up later, "he said.

"Okay, I said, but where? We don't know anywhere." We both laughed at the same time.

"There must be an English pub on the main strip that plays Only Fools and Horses constantly," he replied with a giggle and another amazing smile.

"Okay," I replied I'll keep a lookout.

"I'm Steven, by the way."

"I'm Nicky; nice to meet you."

Chapter 13

AS WE GOT into the terminal building, we made our way to the baggage carousel. Fitty, I mean, Steven and his mates made their way to the other end, and I kept glancing over, couldn't help myself. After about 20 minutes, the carousel started and cases and prams began moving round. Mine was a black suitcase, and my dad had put a rainbow-coloured strap around it so it would be easy for me to recognise it, he had told me. Cases passed me by sometimes twice, but no sign of mine. I started worrying about my case going missing and ending up in Spain or somewhere. Sharon had hers, so I thought I could use her stuff at least. Eventually, I recognised the rainbow strap and grabbed the case off the carousel, banging my shin at the same time. Great, I thought a lovely bruise for the beach!!

We made our way out of the terminal, and I felt like a sweaty mess. It was organised chaos! Reps from all different travel companies waving boards in the air with the company name on. It was then that I heard loud music coming from a group of people and the embarrassing sight of the Club 18-30 reps standing there with clipboards. I looked at Sharon and thought oh shit hope no one sees us!

We reluctantly made our way to a dark-haired girl with bunches in with illuminous green bobbles and bright red lipstick. "Club 18-30," she said in a cockney accent.

"Yes," I replied. I gave her my surname and she told us to go to coach number 11. She was totally over the top, and I felt ashamed for her.

As we stepped out of the terminal, the sun shone in my eyes and nearly blinded me. It was only 10:30 a.m., and it was already boiling hot. I loved the heat, but this was going to be a hot one. I put on my sunglasses and made our way to the coach stop. We made our way to Coach number 11, and it was almost full. I think they were only waiting for us. We waited 15 minutes, then the rep got on, and the engine started up, and thankfully, so did the air conditioning.

"Hello guys," said a jolly-sounding man, who looked like a right divvy. I'm Chris, and I am going to be one of your reps for the next two weeks. Chris looked like a budget version of Jason Donovan. He shouted out various surnames to ensure we were all present and correct.

Once the school register was done, we were on our way. The people on the coach were dead rowdy and loud. A gang of lads at the back started singing Charlie had a pigeon. I remembered this from school trips; it was quite funny, actually. I was by no means a shrinking violet, but this lot were another level. The rep had put the Vengabus song on the coach radio, all the dickheads cheered!

Chris went through the usual bullshit telling us the duration of the journey and the main tourist attractions that they recommend we visit while we were on the amazing island of Crete. It was then that he mentioned the excursions that he recommended to us and that we could book for a "really amazing price" if we booked with them. At this point, he mentioned the infamous "Welcome Meeting" that we must attend in the morning so that they can check our passports! Ha I knew this was a load of bullshit just to get us to book these amazing excursions. I'd already been warned about this. All I wanted to do at this moment was get to my apartment, sort of unpack and get some cooler clothes on as I was about to self-combust. My bra was sticking to me, and all I wanted to do was take it off, but obviously couldn't as I'd look like a boy.

As I had predicted our apartment was the last drop off. As we pulled up outside I was greeted with a cute looking little place with trees at the front with olives growing on them. I hated Olives but I could foresee a drunken night picking them off the tree and eating them one night.

We were greeted by a lovely man with Sunkissed skin wearing a white vest and denim shorts, he was in his 50s, but he had a lovely smile. He showed us to our room which was on the 2nd floor. His name was George obviously the owner of Georgios apartments!

He told us the rules and regulations that mainly consisted of no guests after midnight (yeh yeh) and that the water was turned off also at midnight, so if we needed any to fill up a pan, for example. I asked him why, and he explained how expensive and valuable the fresh water supply was. The main rule that made me shudder was to put no toilet paper down the toilet and put it in the bin next to it!! How disgusting, I thought, but he also explained the plumbing was years old and would get easily blocked. As we arrived at the front door of our apartment, he opened the door for us and then handed me the key. He said his goodbyes, smiled and made his way back down the cold stone stairs. He seemed a really nice fella.

Hopefully we wouldn't piss him off in the next 2 weeks.

It was quite spacious, and I was pleasantly surprised. As you walked in there was a large living area with minimal furniture and then a separate kitchen and a bedroom with 2 single beds in.

Sharon dragged her case into the bedroom and claimed the bed closest to the door so I was left with the one by the window, that I was secretly happy with as I could get a breeze from the window or get eaten to death by the mosquitos. There was one wooden wardrobe with 7 metal coat hangers in mostly bent out of shape. We hung both our jackets on one and dived the others between us. Looked like we had to quadruple hang our clothes then or leave in the case. Most probably the latter.

It was now just before 2 pm, at first we thought it was 12, but then we realised Greece was 2 hours ahead. It was absolutely boiling. We hung a few bits up and then got changed into some shorts and a vest top. When I opened my case, I found two bars of dairy milk hidden under my clothes. I knew that was my dad; he always used to leave cute presents. When I was young, my dad was Bluebell the fairy and left me notes around the house in beautiful fountain pen writing. I think I was 12 before I realised it was my him, I was so naïve, but I didn't care, it was lovely.

We were sweaty, smelly and tired but we decided to have a little explore of our area to see where the main strip of bars was so we could get our bearings and to pick up some groceries for the room and some booze for later.

We walked into the scorching sun again, and immediately I felt the burn of its rays on my shoulders. I'd been on the sunbeds for a few sessions in the few weeks leading up to the holiday and thought I was quite tanned, but in this light, I looked ill, not one bit brown. Shit, I had not put any suntan lotion on I thought. Oh well, we won't be out for long. We walked out of the apartment complex and saw a gang of girls who also looked like they were staying at the same place as us. They were laughing and shouting and I listened in and heard something about shagging and condoms! I felt embarrassed and amused by their conversation, which I was discreetly listening to. We turned left and walked for about 10 minutes past a supermarket and some tavernas serving the local delicacies. It was quiet at this time, hardly anywhere open as it was siesta time. "Only mad dogs and Englishmen go out in the midday sun," I had heard my mum preach on numerous occasions. I agreed with her at this moment, the sun was almost unbearable!

We decided to head back via the supermarket. We got bottles of water, Fanta lemon, crisps that looked like Wotsits, bread that was rock hard even though it was supposed to be fresh and a bottle of ouzo because it was dirt cheap. We were going to go back and have a sleep and then go out in the evening, about 8 pm. I was secretly looking for any English bars so that I could try and meet Steven aka Fitty, but I didn't see any. I was sure I would stumble by one later. All I wanted at this point was to crash out on my bed and sleep; we were both exhausted.

Chapter 14

WE WOKE UP about 7:30 p.m., and I felt like I had been in a coma. I was groggy and weird. Surely you didn't get jetlag after a 4-hour flight! I think we were lucky to actually wake up. I think the noise from the bar downstairs had woken us. It might be a good alarm clock for the next 14 days.

I had crashed out in my clothes, and when I took my vest off to get into the shower, I had bloody strap marks already. I'd only been in the sun for about an hour. Got to layer the sun lotion on tomorrow, I thought.

The shower was a sight to behold. It had no curtain and was basically a shower head that hung from the floor that you had to hold above your head yourself, with a few bits of green in between the tiles. I just hoped there was hot water. It was lukewarm, but it actually felt nice as it woke me up, and it was quite humid in our room. There was one bath towel and one hand towel that were threadbare, but I did not care at all. Then came the effort of drying my hair with the hairdryer. It was still about 25 degrees. My hair was naturally curly, but I tried to blow it straight. Where's my dad with the iron when I need him?

I started the arduous process of hair drying, but 5 minutes into the job, I realised this was not going to turn out as I wanted. So, I decided to use a hair clamp at the back, straighten my fringe to the best of my ability, and layer it with hairspray. I decided to wear cropped jeans as my legs were still snow white and a frilled black top with thick straps to hide the stupid marks that I had got earlier.

All the time I was getting ready, I was thinking if I would bump into Steven. I hadn't mentioned it to Sharon because I knew she would get a gob on if she thought I was going to leave her out for a boy. And considering it was our first night, I had no intention of copping off with anyone, but it would be nice to see him and get to know him a bit better. Hopefully, he would have a nice mate for Sharon.

We eventually left our apartment at about 8,45 after we had forced two ouzo and Fanta lemons down our throats. It was disgusting but got you pissed quickly and it was dirt cheap. We worked out that a bottle of the local stuff was about £3.00. We were greeted by the smell of the local restaurants, which suddenly made us realise we hadn't eaten since the plane. We walked for about ten minutes and settled on a taverna called Dino's that looked nice but reasonably priced. We were greeted at the entrance by a man dressed in a white shirt and black trousers who guided us to a table for two. So far, all the men looked the same. He gave us a menu each and walked away. I decided on spaghetti Bolognese, and Sharon ordered a pizza, and we both ordered a Diet Coke. Obviously, there were Greek meals on offer, but we were both a bit dubious; we didn't want the runs on our first night, now did we, so we decided to play it safe.

A few minutes later, the friendly waiter we had learnt was called Yannis, brought us a jug of water and two glasses. All of a sudden, a warning from my mum sprang into my head. Do not drink the tap water; it will upset your tummy! So, I stuck to my Diet Coke. So many things to think about being abroad. The food arrived shortly after, and we ate as if it were our last meal on death row!! As we were sitting in the taverna, we noticed loads of people all dressed up heading into the main area where the bars were. We started getting excited and started eyeing up any potential suitors.

It was just before 10 p.m., and we were ready for action. We paid our bill and were given a free shot of ouzo. This was knocked back with a following shudder! The warm, fuzzy feeling and the burning sensation down my throat had returned.

Sharon started getting louder as usual, so the ouzo had the desired effect. We walked for a few minutes and started being greeted by various bars, each playing different songs, so it was a blur of noise and bright lights. And then the attack of the bar touts. They were like fly's round shit, each one offering different free drinks and deals if you came into their bar. It was so confusing, a little intimidating, and definitely irritating. We politely declined a few, and a few got told to piss off.

We eventually decided on Romeo's, which seemed quite busy. It had good music and offered two-for-one drinks and two free shots, probably petrol, but we didn't care. We just wanted to get pissed and try and forget how tired we were. Secretly, if Sharon had said shall we go back to the apartment, I would have bitten her hand off as I wasn't in the mood.

I was still keeping an eye out for an English bar playing Only Fools and Horses, but no luck so far. And then about half an hour later, after two shots of ouzo and buying one and getting one free vodka and coke, I didn't even care. We were having such a laugh - you know them silly times when even the slightest things amused you. We stayed here for a bit, then made our way further down the strip, and by this time, it was nearly midnight. It was wall to wall people, and mostly all drunk. I think we lasted about another two hours, and then we I suddenly hit a wall. It was time for bed. We would go for it properly tomorrow night, we decided. And I would definitely look for an English bar!

Chapter 15

I WOKE UP early because the room was like a sauna, and I was dripping in sweat. I must have practically passed out last night, so the heat hadn't bothered me. We had that stupid welcome meeting this morning at 11 am. The Jason Donovan lookalike rep told us we need to be there as we must have our passports and return tickets checked. What a load of crap, it was just an excuse to get us there. But at the back of my mind, I was a little bit scared just in case we did need our tickets checked, so I woke Sharon up and reminded her we had to attend.

The meeting was in a bar a few doors down from our apartments, so it wasn't a big hassle. As we approached the venue, all we could hear was loud music: "Groove is in the Heart" by Deee-Lite. I did love this song, but not at 11 am with a slight hangover!

On the way to the meeting, I found a phone kiosk. I'd promised my mum I would ring her to let her know I had got there safely. I should have done this yesterday, oops! For the life of me, I couldn't remember the code for England. Luckily, the girls we saw the other day were just finishing their call and reminded me it was 0044 and to take the 0 of the area code. I had two 100 Drachma coins and a load of slummy left from last night. I waited for the dialling tone, which confused me as it was different from back home, and then keyed in the number slowly. Eventually, I heard a weird ringing tone, and my mum answered. Our conversation was rushed as I wasn't sure how long my money would last, so I told her I was safe, how hot it was, etc. She told me the cat and Sally the dog were missing me and that they had liver and bacon for tea last night, my favourite—ridiculous information. Oh, and also told me off for not ringing her yesterday. She said she almost contacted Radio City and the Echo! Imagine the embarrassment.

As we walked into the meeting, it was half full and we were greeted with an over-the-top hello from Jason Donovan and another girl with those stupid illuminous pigtails. Stupid cow wound me up already. We found a seat near the back so we could hide away. I didn't want to be at the front to be picked on or whatever they would do. After all, this was club 18-30, and their reputation was infamous. The bar stunk of stale beer and piss. I looked at Sharon and gave her a look. She knows my look.
The annoying girl approached us and handed us two shots of ouzo each. "Hi girls, I'm Donna, and I'm your rep for the Georgios apartments"

"Great," I said sarcastically and gave her the look I had just given Sharon. The thought of drinking the ouzo made me want to vomit but I had to do it so I could erase Donna and the smell of piss from my senses.

Roughly about 5 minutes later I felt pissed again. I'm sure at one point I hugged Donna and told her I am so happy she's my rep, what a lying bitch I am.

To cut a long story short, Sharon and I ended up booking a 'bar crawl and a booze cruise. We stopped ourselves from booking a trip to Spinalonga Island at the last minute. We parted with one hundred drachma between us for both trips, and we were given little bits of flimsy paper with a confirmation receipt of each trip. The Bar Crawl was tonight and started at 8 pm at a bar next to our apartments. We were promised free drinks in each bar along with free shots along the way.

I could not believe the lies I had told myself about not having any involvement with Club 18- 30 and there I was just over 24 hours later giving them my money and falling for all their crap. Oh well, when in Rome, I thought, or Crete on this occasion. When we left the meeting, it was midday. I was dying to get to the beach so I could start my tanning process. Sharon and I already had our bikinis on under our clothes, and we had our beach bags and tape player with us. We made our way to the beach, which luckily was only a few minutes away.

It was a lovely sandy beach, and it was already full. You could hire a sunbed to lie on daily, but they were all taken by this time. My friend from Labellos had told me to put my towel on a sunbed as early as possible to guarantee a space. I'll try this tomorrow, but I wasn't going to pay 20 Drachma every day. So, we had a stroll down the beach and found a nice spot to put our straw beach mats and Lilo's on with our beach towels over. We were lucky as a couple of the girls we had seen yesterday were going home that night, so they gave us two beach mats and two Lilo's. It was a weird feeling taking my top and shorts off in public to reveal my bikini. Realistically, I thought it was like wearing my knickers and bra, but it was so hot that the thought soon disappeared. We set up camp and then started the arduous process of putting suntan lotion on. We did each other's backs and the rest ourselves. It was boiling. We had a bottle of water from the supermarket and the Wotsits-type crisps.

The view was amazing. Crystal clear blue water flowing up towards the sandy beach with the coast on either side, an array of white and blue houses, and the mountains in their full glory in the distance. There was also a nice view of some boys to our left with their ghetto blaster playing Phil Collins. I'd forgotten to bring the mix tapes for our tape player, but probably for the best, as the noise would have been annoying from two different sets of music, even though I had one of my Phil Collins tapes with me.

We lay down and it was slightly uncomfortable, so I shifted my bum and back around a bit so I could get as comfortable as possible. I kept a lookout for anyone leaving their paid-for sun loungers so we could pounce and pretend we were the original customers. We lay there next to each other and chatted for a bit, mainly discussing the plan of attack for tonight and what we were going to wear. We decided to eat in our apartment tonight because we were conscious of spending our money too quickly. Plus, we had to be out slightly earlier tonight because we had the fantastic, wonderful Club 18-30 bar crawl. Oh god, I thought about what we had let ourselves in for!!

Soon after, I must have fallen asleep, and God knows how long it lasted. When I woke up, I felt like I was in a daze, and it took me a moment to come around. I then realised I had been asleep for over two hours—talk about a power nap! Sharon was still asleep and made me laugh as her mouth was wide open, catching flies. She came round after about ten minutes, mainly because I emptied the end of our water bottle over her face! She jumped up and we laughed. I thought this holiday was going to be so much fun. We chatted for a while and planned our evening. By now it was nearly 5.00 pm, so we decided to pack our things up and make our way to the supermarket to get stuff for our tea, and some ouzo and Fanta, obviously.

We decided on crusty bread with cheese and crisps, which was very posh. We hadn't looked in the cupboards in our apartment's kitchen properly, so we didn't know if we even had any cooking items, so we decided on cheese sandwiches with crisps and some massive tomatoes that smelled divine. We just wanted stodge, and we were absolutely starving. We also picked up a couple of postcards and stamps each to send home. We would probably arrive home before them, but it's the thought that counts.

We had to be ready for 8.00 to meet the reps and the other mugs who had booked the club 18-30 bar crawl. We sat on our balcony and ate our cordon bleu meal, washed down with ouzo and lemon, with the accompanying shudder. We started to write our postcards. I was only sending one to Mum, Dad, and Grandad. Said the usual, "the weather is great, wish you were here," which was a complete lie. By the time I decided to have a shower, I was half pissed. We put on a tape and had a little get-ready party, it was a right laugh. I caked myself in after sun and felt all glowing as if I had caught the sun, and it felt nice. Steven popped into my head again, and I wanted to know whether I would meet up with him at all.

He was gorgeous and I wouldn't mind a snog or more, but I placed it to the back of my head and concentrated on tonight.

It was 7.45, and we were ready to rock and roll. I wondered what tonight would bring. I was determined to get a snog, hopefully from Steven, but at this point, anyone half decent would do. Let's have another ouzo first, though, I thought! I was quite excited.

Chapter 16

WE LEFT THE apartment, almost falling down the stone stairs at one point. The fresh air must have hit us, and our ouzo had the desired effect.

The bar crawl meeting point was at a bar called Electric, about one minute from our apartments, as promised. We walked towards it, and it seemed quite busy already. Then I saw Dizzy Donna (I'd nicknamed her); she looked like a Christmas tree with plaits. She was dressed up in a tight green dress (illuminous obviously), red knee-high socks and white high heels. And Jason Donovan looked gorgeous, I was definitely pissed. I wondered how long it would take me to start singing Especially for You to him. Probably not long knowing me when I'm drunk.

We were greeted with an embarrassing whoop whoop as we walked in, which made me shudder. As we walked towards the bar, a shot of something was thrown at us as we were asked for our ticket. We handed it over and did the shot. Oh my god, my throat and chest started burning, definitely petrol or something along those lines. The bar crawl had promised a free drink in every bar, with shots and drink prizes along the way. I could only imagine what the prizes would be for.

The music was blasting, and it was getting busier and busier by the minute. We both felt quite shy at first, as there were a few gangs of girls and boys and a few smaller groups. We ended up standing by two girls from Middlesbrough, Helen and Julie. We

The Wonder Bra Years

started chatting and immediately hit it off. They must have arrived on the same day and looked as white and red in parts as we did. They seemed to be as horrified as we were that we were here and had actually paid good money for the pleasure.

Half an hour passed, and an almighty siren-type thing was heard all over Electric, and probably in the next town, it was that deafening. Dizzy Donna had a microphone and gave us a five-minute warning that we would be leaving and going to the next bar. That gave us time to go for a wee and reapply lipstick, etc. The toilet was vile, the floor was full of water and piss and no toilet paper so it was a drip-dry situation!

The siren went again, and we were told we were off to the next bar called Broncos. We were told by Donna to get into a line two by two (they could do one, she wasn't Noah) and follow them. We walked for about 5 minutes, and no one was two by two. We arrived at Broncos, and it was a cocktail bar with a Bucking Bronco game in the front.

"Sharon, do not let me get on that, " I exclaimed. I know what I'm like. She laughed and gave me a thumbs-up. We were ushered towards the back, where there were jugs of cocktails and shots of, guess what? Yes ouzo. I grabbed two shots for me and Sharon, and the Middlesbrough girls did the same. I then got another two when no one was watching, probably regret that later when I was vomiting aniseed. I was now well and truly pissed and felt on cloud nine and ready for almost anything but definitely not the Bucking Bronco.

After 10 minutes or so, they announced the first game, and the prize was a jug of the special cocktail. Wow, probably an Ouzo and Petrol cocktail. No way was I doing anything, well, not yet anyway. Julie, one of the Middlesbrough girls, put her hand up, and so did a few boys from the bigger groups, and a cute blond boy was chosen. The game was to fetch an article that the rep shouted out. The first one was a white sock, easy enough. The Blonde boy was first back with that after grabbing it from one of his friends. Then it got a bit more daring. A pair of shorts, a bra, a kiss!!! The game was hilarious, watching the contestants run around trying to get items of clothing off people. There was no way I was taking my bra off; padding would fall out. When the kiss item was shouted, the blond boy ran to me and dragged me to the front and started kissing me, not a peck but a proper open-mouth kiss with tongues - his anyway.

As I was drunk, I obliged, and it was quite nice. As he pulled away, I giggled to myself and looked over at Sharon!! But my eyes did not fall on Sharon, they fell on Steven the fitty from the airport!!! Oh my god, what had I done? He looked me in the eyes, gave me a wink and walked away.

My stomach sunk; I ran after him out of the bar. I heard Sharon shout me but I ignored her, I wasn't interested. "Steven," I shouted and he turned round. "Hi," I said in a sheepish manner. To be honest I didn't owe him an explanation, I didn't even know the lad, but he was nice looking and looked gorgeous. Even more gorgeous than I had remembered.

"See your having a nice time," he said in a sarcastic manner with a bit of a smarmy attitude and a fake laugh.

"It was a game," I replied with an attitude.

"Maybe catch you later," he said as he walked away.

"Yes maybe," I replied, turned my back away and walked back into the bar.

"Where have you been?" Bellowed Sharon.

"Oh just for a bit of fresh air," I replied. I could not be bothered telling her. Also I was a bit embarrassed that I had feelings for someone I didn't even know. Cheeky git, I wasn't going to let a boy who I had known for less than half an hour ruin my night or my holiday! I felt sick to my stomach. I don't know why but there was something about him.

Let the holiday frivolities commence, I thought. And grabbed the blond boy again for round two!

Chapter 17

THE BLOND BOY turned out to be called Sean from Manchester. He was good-looking but not the brightest star in the sky, as I found out trying to form a conversation with him during the night! We spent the rest of our night together snogging, drinking and dancing. He was a sloppy kisser and kept trying to force his tongue down my throat. Sharon had copped off with his mate John, and the four of us had a brilliant night, absolutely smashed from all the shots and Ouzo. We ended up back at their apartment, and I ended up snogging Sean on one bed, and Sharon was snogging John on the other. Nothing else happened, no wandering hands - we were all too pissed, anyway. Eventually, around 5 am, we must have all passed out.

I woke up at God knows what time, but I was sweaty and smelly (again) and had a mouth so dry I would have drunk water from the toilet. And as soon as I lifted my head off the pillow, the headache reared its ugly head.

"Urggggghh," I mouthed, feeling a bit sick come up. "Sharon, are you awake?" I whispered.

"Urggggghh, yes," she moaned back.

"Come on, let's go," as I attempted to rise from the dead.

As I moved, I felt a hand wrap around my waist, and Sean attempted to kiss me. As I turned to look at him, I thought, good God, he's vile! A Netto version of Jason Donovan. I definitely had my Ouzo goggles on last night. One of his eyes looked one way and the other looked the other way.

"Last night was great," he whispered as he tried to cuddle me, which made me cringe; I was going to be sick.

"Yes," I said, "but I'll have to go now. We have an excursion booked." God, I'm such a good liar when required.

"Ok," he said, "Can we meet up later?"

I didn't know what to say, I didn't want to come across as a total bitch but there was no way I was going there again, not even if he was the last person on earth and the worlds fertility rates depended on me.

"OK, I'll see you on the strip later," I said, as I stood up and grabbed my shoes. I gave Sharon a nod and we scarpered as quickly as we could. As we got out of their apartment complex we looked at each other and pissed ourselves laughing!!
And then my stomach sank as I remembered bumping into Steven. I made it my mission to find him tonight and try and work my charms, but first a pint of Coke, two paracetamol and sleep.

As we did the walk of shame back to our apartment wearing last night's clothes, mascara all under our eyes and our shoes in our hands, Sharon suddenly stopped in front of me and grabbed my shoulders. "Oh my God, Nicky, have you seen your neck?"

"No, why?" I wondered. I looked in the wing mirror of a parked car, and there was a bloody, bright red love bite!

I wanted to die there and then on the spot!! Oh, bloody hell what a dickhead that Sean was and what an idiot I was for being so pissed that I didn't even realise that Count Dracula had been sucking on my neck.

Oh my God, Steven! How the hell was I going to worm my way into his affections now with a bloody big mark on my neck? The situation called for Operation Concealer, but not till after I had had a few hours' sleep and painkillers for the almighty hangover that was creeping in more and more as the time went on.

Chapter 18

I WOKE UP in another coma-like state after about four hours of sleep. The time was 1 pm, and I still felt awful. Sharon and I got back to our apartment around 9 am and went straight to bed, didn't even have a wash or clean our teeth, absolute tramps. I staggered to the bathroom to swill my face with water to wake myself up and then NOOOOOOO!!!, this round raging red circle greeted me in the mirror at the left-hand side of my lower neck. I had a hickey from Kenickie from Grease! Well, I was in Greece but Oh well you know what I mean!!

Right keep calm I said to myself, trying to remember all the old wife's tales of how to remove or lighten the effects of a love bite. Toothpaste!! I remembered that. So, I killed two birds with one stone and cleaned my disgusting ouzo silk cut breath, teeth and tongue and rubbed Colgate on the offending item and left a big blob on there to soak in and hopefully do what I'd heard it's supposed to.

I walked back into the bedroom and Sharon was awake and took one look at me with a blob of white stuff on my neck and proceeded to almost piss herself laughing. "What the fuck am I going to do" I cried! In between her bouts of uncontrollable laughter Sharon informed me there was sod all I could do but wear a polar neck jumper. "Oh, aye yeh I'll wear the polar neck I packed to wear in 90 degrees heat!!! However, I did remember packing a halter neck top, so at least I had one option.

We freshened up and got our beach stuff together. On the way though we needed food, I felt like I was going to pass away due to starvation.

Georgios, our apartments, had a little bar that served food on site, so we went down and ordered a cheeseburger and chips with a pint of full-fat Coke. We were the only ones there, so it didn't take long; every other sensible person without a love bite was already sunning themselves on the beach. I still could not believe I'd been so stupid or that drunk. Oh god I hope I wasn't going to bump into simple Sean that night, he was as thick as pig shit and a rubbish kisser.

I stuffed the burger and chips into my gob as if I was going for a world record. I'd always wanted to go on Record Breakers as a kid, loved Roy Castle and Norris McWhirter but don't think eating a burger and chips in two minutes would qualify somehow. It was usually just full of bloody tap dancers.

After our food we headed to the beach. By this time there were some sunbeds free as it was quite late in the day and they had already been paid for. We crashed out again as soon as we settled into our plastic wire sun loungers with our towels. We had no energy to carry mats and inflatables today. I was careful to place my hair to one side over the love bite as best as I could. Sun lotion was applied, and a bottle of water was at our sides. Every time I thought about last night and seeing Fitty, my stomach flipped, and the sick feeling returned. I soon drifted off to sleep, listening to the waves crashing onto the sand, and a gentle breeze was hitting my face.

After our second power nap of the day, we headed back to the apartment to start getting ready for tonight, and we both vowed not to get as drunk as last night, so we didn't end up with any gremlins. We had also decided to go out for a proper tea, so we could line our stomachs, because that bloody ouzo was lethal, but it was cheap, and even though we were only a few days into our holiday, we were conscious of running out of money. We had to hide our money in the apartment as we could not really afford a safety deposit box. So, we came up with an amazing hiding place in our pillowcases, genius or what.

Sharon was first in the shower, so I used my time to try and find a suitable item of clothing to hide my neck. As I had previously thought, the halter neck top was my best and only option. Soon it was my turn to freshen up and wash my hair. It was a nightmare drying my hair with the hairdryer as it was so humid and any attempt at trying to blow dry it straight was practically pointless, so as I had done the night before, I dried it as best I could and threw it up with a clamp at the back and loads of Insette. I put a few strands from the clamp on either side of my face as another deterrent, so the love bite was hidden, and also with the straps of my top and some strategically applied foundation and concealer, I was onto a winner, or so I thought.

We were ready just after 8.30 and we decided to go back to Dino's taverna that we went to on our first night. We trusted it as we didn't get the runs after eating there the first time.

This time I decided to have Souvlaki, a traditional Greek dish, and Sharon, for a change, had a pizza! We decided to try and look civilised, so we ordered a carafe of house wine. Well, that was an experience. If you can imagine drinking toilet duck with a hint of Sarrsons vinegar, then you pretty much have an idea of the taste. It was disgusting but potent. We ordered a lemonade to weaken the taste, and because we had paid for it, we drank the lot. And lo and behold, I was absolutely smashed again. Oh dear, I thought to myself, please try and behave.

All I can say is my thought process unfortunately didn't last long. Bloody Malia!!!.

Chapter 19

"OH GOD, I want to die," I mouthed to Sharon!! I had just puked my brains out in the toilets of Dino's. That bloody wine had hit me as soon as I stood up from our table. I was beginning to wonder if I had some fatal disease that was making me sick. Did I hell it was too much cheap booze; my insides will be rotting away as I speak. God knows what I will be like at the end of the fortnight. Dead probably.

It was a highly impressive vomit, I must say so myself. The projection of it was something Roy Castle and Record Breakers would definitely consider seeing, as I probably wouldn't win the burger-eating record. The toilet was the worst I had seen, and I had seen a few nasty ones in the last couple of days, and I had just single-handedly made this one even worse. I decided I would never complain to my dad again when I found his moustache trimmings in the sink at home. I tried to fix my face in the mirror and had a Juicy Fruit to freshen my spew breath.

We went into the next bar, which looked busy, and the music was good. As we walked in, it was playing Pump Up the Jam. Sharon ordered us an ouzo and Fanta again, with another free shot of God knows what. I wasn't sure whether I could stomach more ouzo, but I had a good go. The bartender handed us the shots, and as a fool, I grabbed mine and swigged it down. Approximately 10 seconds after that, I started to feel weird and ran to the toilet again. The toilet stank of piss, but I didn't care, I ran to the nearest sink as the two cubicles were occupied. This is when another projectile masterpiece occurred. However, as soon as I had finished, I immediately felt better.

"It makes a change, being you and not me," Sharon giggled.

"Ha, I know. Anyway, let's crack on," I said, feeling marvellous. I reapplied my lipstick, had another juicy fruit chewing gum, and walked out of the toilets.

As I walked out there, he was. Steven. My stomach sank, and I felt sick. He looked gorgeous. He wore a Ralph Lauren t-shirt with cream shorts and a fantastic tan. And there I was puking my brains out. Suddenly, he grabbed me towards him and started kissing me, and this time, it was one of the most amazing kisses I had ever had. It felt amazing, and he wrapped his arms around my neck and pulled me as close to him as possible. Eventually, I pulled away and gazed into his eyes. "I, I'm, but," I couldn't get my words out. What I wanted to say was sorry my breath must stink of shit because I have just vomited everywhere.

"Well, that was nice," he whispered. I wanted to agree, but I still couldn't speak, and this was a first for me; I usually have verbal diarrhoea, according to my mum.

"Let me tell you about the other night," I managed to say, "It was a game, the stupid club 18-30 pub crawl had dares, and I was picked" I went on. I needed to explain to him.

"So that was it, just a kiss for a game," Steven answered.

"Yes, honestly," I replied. God forgive me for lying, but it wasn't a proper lie, it was a whitish lie!!

"Okay, forget it. Let's go and have a good night," Steven replied, smiled, and grabbed my hand in the main area of the bar when one of my favourite songs was playing, Criticise by Alexander O'Neill. It felt like a moment I would remember forever. As we walked into the bar, I spotted Sharon playing tonsil tennis with some guys. "See, your mate has made friends with Ryan," Steven said. "He's one of my mates," he laughed.

This night was turning out to be amazing.

The rest of the night went from amazing to out of this world. Steven and I danced, laughed, and had the same warped sense of humour. We kissed almost all night. Sharon and Ryan rarely separated themselves from each other's mouths, either. It's great when you cop off with someone you like, but even better when your best mate gets with his mate. It makes life a whole lot easier.

It got to about 2 a.m., and we started to make our way towards the beach. It was still really warm, and you could hear the tide coming up towards the sand like it had earlier, but this time, it was romantic and not sending me to sleep. I longed for romance. I was a big softy at heart. All I wanted was the classic Mills and Boon love story with a dashing man who sweeps the girl off her feet—well, off her flipflops, in this case.

We staggered onto the beach holding each other's hands and walked along for a few minutes until we arrived at the same place where I was sunbathing earlier. We sat on a sun lounger that felt slightly damp as the night air was cooling. We started kissing again and eventually lay down beside each other. Steven was such a fantastic kisser, no tongue down my throat, and I could feel myself falling for him even though I'd only properly known him for a few hours. My chin was beginning to get sore from his stubble, but I didn't care; I could do this all night. Steven was a gentleman. His hands were around my waist or shoulders, and he didn't let his hands wander. Part of me was slightly disappointed, but the other half had a feeling this was something special, and I wanted him to respect me. After an hour or so, it started to cool down, and we were exhausted and beginning to nod off.

"Come on," Steven said, "I'll walk you home."

Chapter 20

AS THE SUN peeped through the flimsy curtain next to my bed, the next morning, I could feel the heat on my face. I felt like Snow white when she wakes up with all the little animals and birds around her. I was so happy. And the best thing was Steven didn't notice the love bite on my neck, thank God for alcohol and halter neck tops. He had walked me to my apartment door earlier this morning, and we arranged to meet on the beach the next day at 11am. I asked him if he wanted to come in for a "coffee" even though I didn't have any, but he politely declined, kissed me on the forehead, and said, "I don't like coffee," and laughed. As he walked away from my apartment door, he turned before he went downstairs and blew me a kiss. I pretended to catch it. What's happening to me? Is this what love feels like?

I looked towards Sharon's bed, and there was no sign. Where the hell was she? I could only assume she went back to Ryan and Stevens' apartment. I just hoped she was ok and had been careful, if you know what I mean. We were both on the contraceptive pill, but you had to think about diseases and aids, especially. I must have dozed off again, but I was woken with a bang at the door. I jumped up, startled; I didn't know where I was for a second. I opened the door to what I can only describe as my best friend, who looked like she had been dragged through a hedge. Or should I say shagged?

"Love is in the air, everywhere I look around" Sharon sang as she skipped into the apartment once again with her shoes in hand.

"Come on," I said, "spill the beans, what happened, and where have you been?" I questioned.

"Well," she started." After you left us, we went back to his apartment, and well," she started to blush.

"You didn't," I said

"Yes, I did," she answered coyly, and it was wow!! I really like him, Nicky.

"Sharon," I shouted, "I hope you were careful," I said in a caring manner.

By the look of her face, she hadn't been. I didn't want to push any further at this moment, but this was a conversation I would continue later. She attempted to change the subject by asking how my night had been. I just gave her a look and she tutted. She knew the look I gave when I really fancied someone. The last time I had this look was when I fancied the lifeguard at the local swimming baths.

I looked at my watch and it was 10.30 am so I had to start getting ready to meet Steven. Shit, I thought how I would disguise the love bite. I went to the mirror and inspected it and luckily it had faded a bit and I could probably pass it off as form of birthmark. I was probably kidding myself!

I mentioned the beach date to Sharon, and she was aware of it, as Steven was at his apartment when she got up, and told her he was meeting me. It was probably the last thing she wanted to do but she knew there was no way she would let me go alone. Also, I think she wanted to see Ryan again, even though she had only just left him just over an hour ago.

I opened my case and searched for the nicest bikini I had. I settled on a black strapless one (padded and underwired, obviously) with high leg briefs. I still didn't have a tan, just a few white lines, so black was my best bet, and the knickers held my stomach in. I tied a bright pink sarong around my waist, got the rest of my beach stuff together, and put a bit of concealer on my neck just in case. I also had a nice pair of jelly shoes in cerise, pink, so I put them on too. They were very colour coordinated, I proudly thought. My hair was given a quick brush, and I put a hair slide in the side that had some kind of fabric flower attached to it, pink obviously.

We had arranged to meet by the sunbeds that we had snogged on the night before. We left our apartment just after 11am and walked towards the beach via the supermarket to pick up water and crisps as usual. I didn't want to look too keen even though I would have run as fast as Linford Christie to get there. We walked for a few minutes, and I saw Steven standing by a wall by the beach at our meeting point. He looked as gorgeous as ever. He was in blue swimming shorts and no top. I couldn't stop looking at his chest. He had a few hairs in the middle that went down to his groin, and he looked perfect. I couldn't believe my luck that he was waiting for me. Skinny ish, no tits me with no tan and a hidden love bite. The worst part was that my hair was naturally curly, so after sweating last night, I looked like Louis 14th.

"Hello, you," he said as I walked towards him. My stomach flipped with excitement. I really liked this boy, and I hoped the feeling was mutual. Ryan was already on the beach with a bucket hat over his face, and as we walked towards him, Sharon's face turned white. Probably because they had slept together last night, and she was feeling a tad embarrassed. I still hadn't spoken to her about it, I would save that for later when we were on our own.

We settled on our sunbeds that the lads had paid for the day. I lay on the one next to Steven and Sharon lay next to Ryan and I could definitely sense awkwardness between them. I had brought the cassette player down to the beach and got my tapes out of my beach bag.

"What you got on these?" Steven enquired. I so wanted him to like me on every level, so I hoped he liked my music. "Any Phil Collins or Genesis?" he asked. Hallelujah, I thought, I had the No Jacket Required tape by Phil Collins with me. As cool as a cucumber, I reached for the tape and placed it in his hands.

"Oh, it's right," Steven said and gave me a cheeky wink. "You are getting better and better." My heart skipped a beat. Things were going so well, I was just waiting for something to go wrong, and I didn't have long to wait. "Right, what do you ladies want to drink?" Steven asked as he stood up.

I was just thinking what to have when I saw Steven staring at me. "What's that on your neck?" He asked with a puzzled look.

I froze and answered suspiciously, "Oh, it's a birthmark, everyone always says it looks like a love bite," I giggled." Steven gave me a look. He knew very well what it was but he didn't question it further.

Shit I thought I am going to have to colour a mark in when the love bite had faded. The situations I get myself into, could only happen to me I thought. We all decided on vodka and freshly squeezed orange juice with the bits in and plenty of ice and a straw.

We had a brilliant day at the beach. We sunbathed for a bit. Steven and I applied each other's sun lotion on our backs. I got goosebumps when he was touching my back, and when his hands moved down towards my bum. He gave it a playful slap, and we both laughed. We swam in the sea and kissed more and more. By this time, my chin was practically raw. I'll have to put some Sudocrem on later, I'm sure I've packed some. Sharon and Ryan were a bit frosty with each other at first. I think that was mostly embarrassment and the fact that neither of them really knew how the other felt, but they relaxed after a couple of vodkas and were chatting and giggling most of the day. I had a gut feeling about Ryan. Something didn't feel right. My gut instinct never let me down in the past, but I put that thought to the back of my head as Sharon seemed to be happy, and it worked out better if we were both with boys who were friends. Nice little double date scenario.

We made plans to all go out for our tea later. Steven said he knew a lovely authentic Greek Taverna and he also promised to take me to the English pub The Red Lion that he had found that played Only Fools and Horses just as he had suggested when we first met.

We left the beach about 4pm and went for a cocktail at the beach bar situated at the top of the beach. I ordered a Pina Colada and so did Sharon. The lads had a pint of lager, typical boys.

After our drinks we went our separate ways and arranged to meet at 8pm at our apartment. Shit, I'll have to have a tidy up I thought. There were clothes everywhere and I'm sure the toilet bin with the poo toilet tissue in needed emptying. Steven turned around again and blew me a kiss and I caught it again.

Sharon and I walked to our apartment via the supermarket and bought some beers (ideal girlfriend material) and the usual shopping list of ouzo, Fanta crisps and bread. We also got some milk so we could have a cup of tea in the morning. I really missed my morning brew. Sorted me out for the day back at home.

By the time we got back, it was after 6pm, so no time for a siesta or disco nap as we had nicknamed it. Before I got in the shower, I did my domestic goddess bit and tidied up the clothes on the floor, threw some in the wardrobe and some under the bed and emptied the toilet bin, one of the worst jobs I had ever done. Sharon's guts were not the healthiest, it appeared. She did tell me several times she had IBS, but I just thought that was an excuse because of the smell.

I jumped into the shower after Sharon and washed my hair and cleaned my body carefully, shaved my legs and armpits and had a little trim of my lady bits. I had a bit of sunburn on my shoulders, and it bloody hurt when the flowing water touched it. I had learnt by now that there was no point blow drying my hair straight as the humidity just made it frizzy and I would practically self-combust drying it as the heat was unbearable and if you got your sunburn with the heat from the hair dryer you knew about it. I had covered myself in after sun and this made me feel a bit cooler.

My fringe had gone reasonably well, so as soon as it was as straight as it could be, I blasted it with hairspray. The rest went back in a loose plait to the side of the love bite. I wanted to look super sexy and gorgeous tonight, and as I now had a bit of a tan, mostly red, I decided on a black off-the-shoulder mini dress that was very fitted. I took the straps off my Wonderbra and put a thong on. God I hated thongs always got stuck up my arse but there was no way I was going to have a VPL (visible panty line for those who don't know). I sorted my makeup, made an extra special effort tonight and had an excitement poo and sprayed some impulse all over the apartment because my nerves were shot but I was looking forward to tonight. I had a gut feeling it was going to be brilliant.

Chapter 21

STEVEN AND RYAN turned up just after 8.15pm with a bottle of vodka and sone fresh orange. They had even acquired a pint glass of Ice from George downstairs. I wasn't usually a big fan of vodka but I had really enjoyed the ones on the beach today. Maybe this is my new drink.

I had the music playing for when they arrived. I daren't put one of my mix tapes on that I had prepared as I wanted to appear cool so I decided on Phil Collins again as I knew this was a sure bet for Steven to like.

The apartment looked as good as it could and we guided the boys into our kitchen area that had a table and two chairs, and we brought the two chairs from the balcony in too. No point really as it was that hot we ended up relocating to the balcony with its cool air and the smell of the evening in Malia which I wish I could bottle up and take home with me. I know that sounds cringy but you just couldn't beat that holiday smell.

We chatted on the balcony for about an hour and gradually got drunk but it was a happy giddy drunk. Roughly about 9.30pm Steven stood up and said, "come on you lot, lets hit the strip." Sharon and I went to the bathroom to top up our makeup and have a wee then we were ready to rock and roll.

The lads asked if we wanted to go for food, but by this point I was past eating. If I ate now, it would make me feel lethargic, and I was in a full-on party mood. I suggested we get a burger later.

Sharon and Ryan walked out of the apartment, leaving me to lock up as I was the sensible one, believe it or not. I almost felt like her carer most of the time! As Steven and I went to lock up, he grabbed me by the waist and told me I looked beautiful. He was either an amazing lad or an absolute bullshitting bastard. He kissed me; it was a lovely, sensual kiss, but all I could think of was him smudging my red lipstick; luckily, I had Lipcote on. I locked up and we walked downstairs to the others. As I walked towards Sharon, she piped up," Fix your lippy, you," and laughed. I knew he would smudge it. I did laugh, though, when I glanced at Steven, and his mouth and chin were full of red lipstick. Lip Cote didn't work as well as it should, I thought to myself.

The rest of the night was the best of my life. Steven and I spent most of the night on our own. We started asking each other about our home lives, jobs and family. Steven was one of three; he had two older sisters. He was a painter and decorator for his dad's company. His mum and dad were separated, but he was still close to both, and according to him, his parents still had quite a good relationship. Like mine, a normal working-class family with good values. I was a bit nervous telling him I only worked in a wine/cocktail bar, but when I was telling him, I did exaggerate my role slightly, practically making myself sound like the assistant manager. Back home, if I was talking to a boy, I used to say I worked as an air hostess for Monarch. It was such a glamorous job, so it always seemed to impress.

We asked each other about ex-partners. I didn't have much to say, really. I had a couple of two/to three-week flings and only one sexual encounter that was highly embarrassing and painful, so I didn't really want to count that as losing my virginity, but I suppose it was. Steven went on to tell me he had had a two-year relationship with a girl from school that he had split up with about 5 months ago. I couldn't help feeling jealous, but I suppose that's only natural if you love someone. WHAT THE HELL! Love someone! Nooooo. Oh shit I was falling for him in a big way but holiday romances never worked. Did they?

We went to a few bars, but the highlight of my night was The Red Lion, an English-style pub. And lo and behold, as soon as we walked in, one of my all-time favourite songs/dances was playing. The Time warp! "Put your hands on your hips and bring your knees in tight," I heard and immediately got into Frank-N-Furter character! I glanced at Steven mid-hip thrust, and he was laughing. See if he wanted me, he had to put up with mad me, the one that occasionally made a show of herself, well more than occasionally, if I was totally honest. Lo and behold, The Red Lion had TV screens on every wall showing Only Fools and Horses but with the volume down. It also had pictures of Dogs playing snooker and Darts behind the bar. So Cliché but brilliant.

For the rest of the holiday, Steven and I were totally inseparable. We spent every day and night together, and I felt like I was really falling for him. We made plans to meet up when we got back to England, and we discussed what we would do and how often we could see each other. I'm not stupid, and I knew all about holiday romances and that things would ultimately change when we got back to normal life. Sharon and Ryan spent time together, too, but I still had reservations about Ryan. Something wasn't right with him. Sharon had brought up seeing him when they got home, but he made excuses like "sort it when we get home" and that kind of stuff.

Before I knew it our last night was here and I felt so emotional. This holiday had been the holiday of all holidays. Id met an amazing man and had a fantastic time and I did not want it to end.

Steven had planned a romantic meal just for the two of us for our last night. Sharon and Ryan would meet us later even though they were probably pissed off but they both knew how we felt about each other. Steven picked me up from my apartment at 7.30pm. Sharon was asleep. I think all her horizontal athletics had taken its toll on her, so she was meeting us at 11pm at the Red Lion, and Ryan was too. They both refused to go out together, but Sharon was happy for a few more hours of rest.

We went to an Italian restaurant that was quite posh compared to some of the places we had been. I loved Italian food. There was an amazing Italian restaurant opposite the bar I worked in back home, and the smell of the garlic always wafted over and made me hungry all the time.

We were guided to our table for two by the waiter. Steven pulled my chair out for me and I sat down. I thought that only happened in films. As we sat at our table waiting to order I kept looking at Steven. He looked so fit. His tan was amazing and he always wore lovely clothes. I was dead fussy about clothes but he always passed my test, never told him that though it was my secret test and he passed with flying colours.

We ordered garlic bread to start, and I ordered Carbonara for main, and he ordered lasagna. As we were waiting, a small Greek man came into the restaurant with a bucket full of roses wrapped in cellophane. Steven called him over and bought me a single red rose. I was cringing at this, as when this happened at home, I always thought it was dead cheesy and a rip-off. He took the rose from the man and placed it in his mouth for a laugh, and smiled. He then handed me the rose and said, "You're really special, Nic, I can't wait to start our adventure back home." I felt my stomach sink, and a tear welled up in my eye. He must have noticed this as he leant over and wiped the tear away. "Pack it in you," he said softly," it will all be ok, you know."

Chapter 22

OUR FLIGHT BACK to Manchester was at 8pm and I woke up in Steven's arms about 10am. "Shit" I shouted as I woke up. I hadn't even started packing my case, and we had to be out of the apartment by 12. I'm sure George would give us some extra time, though.

"Calm down, calm down," Steven said in a fake Scouse accent, imitating the Harry Enfield Scouse characters. I laughed as it was quite a good impression. He grabbed me and started kissing me very passionately, and one thing led to another, and within a few minutes, we were having the most amazing sex I had ever had, even though I wasn't an expert, but this was special.

I read More magazine every time it was released and used to laugh at the Position of the fortnight! Ha however I was far too prudish and shy to attempt to get myself in any of the ridiculous positions that the magazine suggested. I'd probably pull my hamstring.

We were hot and sweaty and this sex really meant something it wasn't just a shag; it was more than that. We were making love. That sounds so pathetic, but I felt so comfortable and safe with him. I wasn't even embarrassed about my small boobs that looked like two fried eggs at the moment as they were so white from my bikini tan lines. It happened so quick we did not even think to use a condom. We had been sensible the other times we had done it, but this time the moment took over and I didn't care. I was on the pill, and I had taken it religiously every day, and he did pull out just in the nick of time. Just be my luck that the only time I hadn't been careful, I'd get chlamydia or something, but surely I'd have an itch by now. I think I already had a bit of cystitis as it really hurt when I had a wee!! I'll sort that when I get home, I thought with the old cranberry juice trick.

Steven got up and jumped into the shower. Sharon returned home then and looked like death warmed up.

"You ok" I said to her.

"Yeh just done in and my fanny hurts," she laughed. We both gave each other a look as if to say wow what a mad time we had had, one not to tell the grandkids in years to come. Or maybe not.

Steven came out of the bathroom with a hand towel over his bits. "How's Ryan?" he asked. Sharon

"I don't know. I ended up in the apartment upstairs with George's son, Andreas."

I was speechless but quite relieved because I didn't like Ryan. It would serve him right if Sharon had left him for someone else.

"He said he would sort it with his dad for us to come and stay here again for half price next year, how good that is, Nic."

Brilliant I thought and what a load of shit. The things men say to get you into bed. I would get the juicy gossip later.

"Right, I'd better get back and pack" Steven said. "Shall we meet up about 1.00pm by the beach and have a few drinks before we get picked up. We were getting picked up at 4pm so there was no point going to the beach we had discussed plus I didn't want to feel dirty and full of sand on the plane.

"Yes, sound," I said. He walked over to me kissed me and pinched my bum. See you in a bit! And we did the usual kiss and catch routine. It was our little thing.

By this time it was nearly 11.15 and I frantically started throwing things into my case. Such a difference from the strategic placing of garments on the way here so I could minimise the creases.

I decided to leave most of my toiletries there for the maids apart from my after sun as I didn't want to peel when I got home. Amazingly we were packed and showered by 12.15. I put a pair of shorts and a t-shirt on with my reebok classics as I was conscious It might be cold when we got back to Manchester, I had a cardigan too in case I got chilly at the airport. I hated being cold I was a right wuss.

We put our cases by the front door and both did the last check of the apartment, like checking drawers and looking under the bed in case we had left anything. I found some of the clothes I had launched under there last week. I was wondering where they had gone.

Shamefully, the only thing I found was a condom wrapper. Thank God I found it before the maid, even though I would never see them again.

We walked down to reception and handed our key to the owner and put our cases in the luggage room until later. We both gave George a hug, he was a lovely man and we told him we would be back soon. It was a fantastic place and It would definitely hold life long memories. Sharon was looking for Andreas but as expected he was nowhere to be seen.

We walked down the beach bar a bit earlier than we had planned to meet the lads as I wanted to have a chat with Sharon about what had happened last night. We got there and ordered a Sex on the beach cocktail, buy one get one free! Result.
Steven and I had already swapped phone numbers and addresses, but when I asked Sharon about Ryan, she said he kept saying I'll sort it later. I had the awful feeing that Sharon was just a shag to him, totally different to what I had with Steven. I could tell she was bothered by it, so I tried to reassure her, telling her "You know what lads are like" etc. Deep down, I had an awful feeling that Ryan was hiding something. A few times I was going to ask Steven about this, but I always forgot or the moment wasn't right. Plus, I was being slightly selfish looking after myself for once, even though I loved Sharon, but sometimes you had to look after number one.

We finished our drink and ordered a jug next; this was also on buy one get one free. I looked at my watch and it was 1.45. Where was Steven? I had a horrible feeling especially as Id slept with him. Here we go I thought, wham bam thank you ma'am!!! This was totally out of character for him. He was always on time. Maybe he was behind on the packing I thought. Yes surely that's it, I hoped.

I could not relax at all and I kept looking up the road to see if he was coming but no sign. We were getting picked up by the airport coach at 4pm and it was now nearly 3pm. Even though I had drunk quite a bit I felt sober as a judge. Sharon was also anxious but she already had doubts about Ryan but I knew Steven was different but I didn't have the heart to say this.

Sod this I thought as it was nearly time to leave, "let's get a few ouzo shots to round the holiday off" I suggested as I stood up to go to the bar.

"Ha why not "Sharon answered. Plenty more fish in the sea Nic!"

Yes there was I thought but I wanted *my* fish.

We had the first shot closely followed by the second and we both shuddered and balked at the same time. We started our holiday on the ouzo and we finished it the same way.

We walked back half pissed to our apartments. I was still looking for Steven but still no sign. The only good thing was that we were on the same flight so he couldn't ignore me. All I could think was the worst.

Surely I hadn't fell for nearly two weeks of absolute bullshit, had I?

Chapter 23

WE STOOD IN the street outside the apartments and sat on our cases waiting for the coach. Eventually about 4.20 the coach arrived with dickhead Donna greeting us. I felt like crying. We gave our cases to the driver to put in the luggage hold and walked onto the coach and managed to get seats next to each other as we were the last pickup. I sat by the window and I didn't say a word and Sharon knew to leave me.

We made our way to the airport with the reps talking their normal shite on the microphone and I just gazed out of the window sad to be leaving such a lovely place and obviously the weather and the feeling of freedom with no worries, no alarms to wake me up and no day- to-day drudgery that happened at home. I loved my job, but the feeling on holiday was second to none. The fact that Steven hadn't turned up made me sad, and I was trying to stay positive, but this was proving harder than I thought. But I was worried and felt sick. What had happened? Has he been hurt, run over on the way back to his apartment, abducted by Aliens?

As we pulled up at the airport entrance my heart skipped a beat as I saw Steven standing by the revolving doors with his suitcase and cassette player in hand. I couldn't believe my eyes. I had to do a double take to make sure it was him, and it was, Id recognise those bright white reebok trainers anywhere. How had kept them so clean I will never know.

Wonder if he is waiting for me. I hoped? Surely he is. Probably just getting fresh air or something. I prepared myself for the usual "It's been great, but!"

Our coach pulled up at the far end of the entrance, and we stepped off into the heat for the last time and made our way to the side of the coach to collect our cases. I felt sick with nerves. What was he going to say? Why didn't he turn up? I dropped my case about three times and scraped my leg again because my nerves were through the roof.

Sharon had also noticed Steven and me could tell she was also looking to see if Ryan was with him, but he wasn't. "Steven is there you know," she said to me.

"I know," I replied. "What shall I say?"

"I'd kick off the cheeky bastard," Sharon scorned. Ha, no way would she say that if Ryan were standing there too. I totally understood her reaction, I would say exactly the same to her if it were the other way round, and I knew she was feeling hurt and humiliated, but it was different for Steven and me, I knew it was. She probably only went with Andreas last night to get some kind of reaction, but I think it had backfired. All it had done was make her feel even more rejected.

I started walking towards the door and Steven must have noticed me and started walking quickly towards me. "Nicky hiya can we talk?" he said. Oh god here we go. I prepared for the worst but I was conscious we had to check in, we could not miss our flight I had work tomorrow.

"Yes," I said, but let us check in first.

The Wonder Bra Years

"Ok," he agreed and followed Sharon and me into the the terminal building, so we could check which desk we had to check in at. We looked up at the board, gate 12 but we were not due to board yet but we had to check our cases in. We headed for the club 18-30 desk and luckily the queue was only small as we were late. Sharon stood in front of me, and Steven stood sheepishly behind me.

"The lads have already checked in, but I waited to check in with you," he said. Is it okay if I sit by you on the plane?
I felt a massive warmth inside. Surely if he was going to end things, he wouldn't want to sit next to me for four hours? Before I knew it, we were at the front of the queue. I passed Sharon, our tickets, and then I handed Steven's in at the same time.
"Smoking or non-smoking?" The check-in assistant asked?

"Smoking," I shouted; I definitely needed a ciggie or ten for the stress. "Do you mind if Steven sits with us" I asked Sharon. She gave me a look; you know that type of look.

"Well, I haven't really got a choice have I but I want the window seat" she snarled.

"Yes okay" I replied like a little girl who had just been told off. She could have had my life savings at this point, not that I had any. I only had a Birmingham Midshires saving account that my dad had started for me when I was younger.

We were handed our boarding cards, and we had three seats together and, thankfully, a window seat.

"Come on girls, let's go and get pissed, my treat, I've got loads of Drachma to get rid of."

If anything was going to break down Sharon's wall of anger, it was free drinks.

We walked towards the escalator and went upstairs to the bar and the duty-free. By this time, it was nearly 6.30, so we did not have long before our flight. We headed towards the bar, and as we walked towards it, we heard a loud "oi oi" from the far side. We looked over and saw Stevens' friends and, of course, Ryan. He was obviously giving Sharon not the cold shoulder but the Antarctic frozen shoulder. I really felt sorry for her, what a bastard, I thought. But I did see him looking over at me. It was weird, I thought!

Steven looked over towards his mates and just gave them a wave. He turned to me and handed me a twenty drachma note and loads of loose change, and said, "Get whatever you want and get me a beer, please" he then walked towards his friends. I ordered a beer and two double Vodka and orange, sod him I though, I was still angry. As I was waiting for the drinks (no ice obviously as I'd get the runs, my mum said), I watched as Steven was chatting to his mates. It seemed like a normal conversation, not a hostile one, but he did seem to be a bit off with Ryan. However, I didn't want to jump to conclusions, as I couldn't hear a word they were saying. I was disturbed by the lady behind the bar gesturing to me to pay for the drinks. I handed her the money, the coins first and then the note and hoped it was enough. Luckily, it was, and I got more change.

Steven walked back over, and we walked towards him with the drinks and made our way to a table by the side that was littered with sandwich wrappers and empty glasses. I cleared our table and placed our drinks down. Steven pulled a seat next to me and grabbed his beer and drank it in one.

"I'm going to duty free," said Sharon as she walked away.

Phew, I thought I needed to talk to Steven. I just hoped I liked what he was going to say.

Chapter 24

AS SOON AS Sharon walked away, Steven grabbed my hand. "Right, you let me explain." I looked at him with a discerning look, preparing myself for the worst. He started to explain that the lads he was on holiday with gave him loads of hassle about leaving them for me on the last day, and for almost all of their holiday, etc. I understood that as we had spent so much time together over the last two weeks. I put myself in his position, and if I had left Sharon practically all holiday for him, there would have been murder. Luckily, it had worked out ok for me for once.

"I had no choice I had to stay with them, I didn't want to but I had too, Im so sorry babe" he explained "And I had no way of letting you know. Also, I've got to tell you about Ryan!"

My heart sank. Not for me, I couldn't give a shit about Ryan, but I was thinking about Sharon.

Steven started to explain that Ryan had a serious girlfriend at home and he had no feelings for Sharon. I bloody knew it! My gut instinct never lets me down. What the hell was I going to say to her?

Steven was rushing through his explanation, knowing that Sharon would be back any minute. "What shall we tell her?" I asked,

"I don't know," he replied.

I started my epic rant!

The Wonder Bra Years

"Well, I think he should tell her the bastard" I was so angry, but I decided to keep quiet and pretend I didn't know anything. "What about us though?" I asked quietly trying to hold back the tears. Im never usually like this but he meant so much to me. Steven grabbed my hand again and gave it a squeeze.

"I've fallen for you big time, Nicky, and I want us to try and make good things at home, if That's what you want"

I tried to act dead, cool, calm, and collected, but my body acted otherwise, and tears welled up in my eyes. I grabbed his face and proceeded to snog the face off him.   "Ditto," I said (I loved that bit of the film Ghost; Patrick Swayze was my dream man, well until now).

Our snog was interrupted by a slamming of a plastic bag at my feet and Sharon standing over us. She knew, I know she knew what was going on but she was putting a very brave face on.

"Steven do me a favour" she started. "Will you tell Ryan I had a great time on holiday but now its home time I don't want anything else" She made this statement with the utmost convincing confidence but I could tell she was dying inside and probably a bit jealous of Steven and I.

"Erm yeh sure love" he replied. It's probably for the best he carried on, "He's always working hardly ever got any spare time" I could tell he was lying but first prize for the best reply possible.

"Right, let's get us another drink before we board and spend all this change," he said as he stood up and walked to the bar. "Double Bacardi's girls?" "No Vodka and orange, please. It's our holiday drink.

"Are you ok?" I asked Sharon as Steven went to the bar.

"No, I'm not, but I've got to be, haven't I?" Sharon looked deflated. "What about Andreas, he's well fit, you must have been made up to cop off with him" "I only did it to try and make Ryan jealous, and it obviously hasn't worked, has it, Nic?" She drank the last bit of her drink in one gulp before Steven walked back towards us with our refill.

"Just do me a favour Nic" she started "don't fuck me off for him when we get home ok, remember chicks before dicks" I laughed at that saying but I promised her I wouldn't, and I meant it. A true best friend was hard to come by, and I'd never sacrifice my friendship with Sharon, even though I was falling in love with Steven. Or had I already fallen? I think you know the answer to this.

Before we knew it our flight was called and we were asked to go to gate 12. Sharon had swigged her drinks practically in one go and I could tell by her face and mannerisms that she was half cut.

"Eh, you," I snarled and poked her in the arm, "act sober when we are boarding, ok?"

"Yes, obviously," she snarled back. I grabbed her arm as we stood up to make our way to the gate.

"Listen, babe, I'm here, you know, don't feel awkward in front of me, ok?" She looked back and gave me a slight nod, and I could see there were tears welling up in her eyes. Poor cow, I thought, I hated men sometimes, well, most of the time.

As we got to the gate, luckily, Ryan and the rest of Stevens' friends were already at the front of the queue, so I was relieved that we didn't have to face them for Sharon's sake. I knew Stevens' friends didn't smoke, so I was also relieved that there was no chance we would be sitting by them. As we got to the front and showed the stewardess our boarding cards, Sharon did her best sober impression, and I'd also given her a piece of juicy fruit chewing gum to disguise any strong alcohol smells. Luckily, I had one piece left.

We made our way up the steps of the plane and soaked in the last few rays of glorious sunshine and that smell that we had become used to. We had three seats near the back, so we walked up the back steps, another lucky escape from Ryan and the rest of the lads. We placed our hand luggage and cassette players in the available spaces in the overhead locker, and I stood aside for Sharon to have the window seat, and then I, and Steven closely followed. Seat belts were fastened, and I lay my head back feeling exhausted due to the stress of the airport and the three double vodkas Id consumed. I was also relieved that our flight wasn't delayed; that was the last thing we needed.

The air hostesses did their usual safety dance, and the captain had a little chat, and then before I knew it, we were off. The engines revved up, and we started moving along the runway, and then the plane sped up, and we were off. I reached out for Sharon's hand as I knew she would be nervous, and I gave it a tight squeeze. My ears never popped on the way up, but they bloody killed on the descent. I always got earache when landing, but I had no Barley sugar or chewing gum left.

I felt sad and happy at the same time. Sad to be going home after an amazing holiday but happy that I had met Seven and was excited for spending more time with him at home. I just hoped it was all going to be plain sailing when we got back to our usual mundane lives.

Chapter 25

WITHIN ABOUT TEN minutes after take-off, Sharon was fast asleep, catching flies with her mouth open and doing the odd snoring noise. I was silently glad about this as it gave Steven and me a chance to talk more about us and what will hopefully happen back home. After a while, the air hostess came round with the drinks trolley and Steven took charge, very masterful, I thought and ordered us a bottle of Champagne. I was in shock! I hadn't had proper Champagne before, only a cheap sparkling wine called Charlemagne at my 18th party that did the job but wasn't the best. I liked most alcohol apart from Martini and gin, bloody disgusting. My school friend and I used to buy the cheap version of Martini called Stock, and we would drink it straight from the bottle in the park!

The hostess came back a few minutes later with the Champagne that had been opened for us and two plastic glasses. He handed me a glass and proceeded to pour both our drinks. He raised his glass to mine and looked me straight in the eye.

"Nicky, I want to make a toast." I started laughing. "Stop it, I'm being serious," he said. My nervous laughter changed almost immediately as I looked straight into his beautiful blue eyes.

"This holiday has been amazing" he started "More than I could have ever imagined and that is because of you" No one had ever spoken to me like this before, it felt like I was in a soap opera or a Hollywood movie. He was either full of shit or I had actual met a knight in shining armour. I was beginning to think the latter.

"Me too," I replied after a massive swig of my sparkles. "But I'm scared this is all too good to be true"

"Well," he started. "We had a bloody good start, and obviously, things won't be as easy as they have been on holiday with work, but I'm sure we can give it a go."

This is where I started thinking more about home and how we could make it work. I mean, I worked weekends, most of the time, and that is when Steven was off work, as he worked in the week. I decided to park those thoughts for now and just go with the flow. We moved towards each other and started kissing. It went on for quite a while until we heard a cough, and the air hostess was next to us with the duty-free trolley.

"Can I get you anything" she asked in a monotone voice.

"No thanks "I said.

Steven piped up "No let me get you something." Oh god he really was perfect. I felt like we were Scott and Charlene from Neighbours. A true love story. I quickly looked at the duty-free brochure from the seat in front and decided on a bottle of Anais Anais. My mum had this and I always borrowed/stole it from her dressing table. I remember my dad telling me the story of going to a department store to buy this perfume for my mum. He wasn't quite sure how to pronounce its name so he said he had roughly asked for Anus Anus thinking he was pronouncing it in French.

Before long, I could smell food and was excited that my evening meal in its foil tray was almost here. I was starving as the Champagne had gone to my head a bit, as we had already had 2 glasses. The food trolley was nearly at our seats, so I gave Sharon a nudge to tell her it was time for dinner. She grunted at me, "Just stick it on my table, I'll have it in a bit," as she turned away to face the window and pulled down the screen to block the light. I'm sure she was annoyed at me, and I was worried about our friendship when we got home. It was hard to find a true friend who understood you and shared the same interests. I'll worry about that when we get home, I thought. Just as the stewardess handed me two sets of food, she handed one to Steven.

I placed Sharon's on her table for later and then opened the hot foil lid on mine and it was some form of meat in a gravy with croquette potatoes and peas with a bread roll and some form of suet pudding with syrup on for pudding. As previously done this was eaten in record breaking time, another attempt at the world record.

"Bloody hell, are you hungry?" Steven laughed.

"Ha," I replied, "If Sharon doesn't wake up soon, I'm having hers as well." He laughed and gave me a playful nudge, and we had another cheer with the remaining bit of Champagne. We had a coffee after finishing the Champagne, reclined our seats, and put blankets on ourselves that the air hostess had supplied for us as we were feeling cold, as she collected our empty glasses and food. I placed half of mine over Sharon as I cuddled up to

Steven under his. Not surprised we were cold as we both had shorts on and the air con was quite chilly. We cuddled up together as best we could with an armrest in the way, with the odd cheeky snog.

We started to discuss when and how we could see each other at home. We were both working, but we couldn't afford hotels all the time, and the train fares would mount up too. I was at work Friday night this weekend and Saturday until 5pm. I suggested that Steven come to me, but we had to sort out accommodation first.

"I'll tell my mum and dad about us and hopefully they will let you stay in mine," I said. I could tell by his face that this made him feel awkward.

"Meeting the parents already," he smirked. "I think the first time we meet, we should stay at a cheap hotel," he suggested.
"Ok, if that's better for you, as long as we see each other," I answered. God I was turning into a right sloppy bitch, I had never been this comfortable with a boy before and I felt like I could say or tell him anything, well almost anything.

We then made plans. When I say I made plans, I mean I blabbed on all kinds of things we could do in Liverpool when he came to stay. Obviously, this included the usual Beatles things and the Liver Birds. When I got home, I would look at the Yellow Pages to try to find a reasonable place for us to stay. I knew the Moat House was nice as I went to the gym there sometimes, but I wasn't sure of the price. There were hotels by Lime Street station, but they were shady. Maybe I would get a discount as I was a gym member. I mentioned The Moat House to him and told him I would make some enquiries tomorrow.

We were due to land in about an hour so I nudged Sharon again, mainly because she was snoring quite loudly this time but also I was trying to suck up to her as I knew she was still going to be upset. She woke up and seemed in a better mood. Steven handed her a vodka and orange as he had caught the stewardess on her way back and ordered more drinks, and she smiled.

"Thanks, Love," she replied and had a good swig. She also had a good attempt at her food; she must have been starving.

"Ladies and Gentlemen," the Tanoy started. It was the captain. "We are starting our descent into Manchester airport; I hope you have had a pleasant flight blah blah" Well, I certainly had.

My mum was picking us up. Id given her the flight number so she was going to check our arrival time on teletext. Stevens's dad was picking him up and two of his mates. I started worrying about Sharon seeing Ryan again in the arrivals hall and how she would react.

Seatbelt and no smoking signs were illuminated, and we started our descent. My ears always hurt on descent, so I grabbed Steven's hand and put my head on his shoulders. We were nearly home. Home sweet home.

Chapter 26

WELL, THAT LANDING was one to remember. There was lots of turbulence and the plane was moving all over the place. My ears hurt so much at one point I had my hands over my ears trying to swallow all the time. Eventually my ears popped and the pain eased considerably. I felt deaf for a good while after. Quite handy as Sharon was on one.

"If I see Ryan when we get our luggage, I'm going to tell him exactly what I feel," she remarked in a very angry tone.

"Oh, Sharon," I started, "don't give him the satisfaction of letting him know you are bothered. Just act like you're not arsed even though I know you are." I gave her a stern look, mainly to let her know that she needed to protect herself from any more heartache.

We let the hustle and bustle of landing die down before we stood up. We got our bags from the overhead lockers and made our way towards the back door of the plane.

Steven and I had already discussed that we would say goodbye properly here so that I could concentrate on Sharon's welfare and keep her from kicking off and he could try his best to keep Ryan out of sight. He was going to call me tomorrow evening at 6pmafter work as by now it was 10.30pm and by the time we got home it would probably be after midnight.

"I'm going to miss you tonight," Steven said as he grabbed my hands. He then proceeded to kiss me, not a full-on snog but a few sensual kisses on my lips.

"Me too," I replied. "I'll miss your sweaty body next to me in the morning," I laughed.

"Cheeky cow, I'll miss your frizzy hair. Ha, speak to you tomorrow at 6pm, ok, I won't let you down, I promise."

Steven started to walk to the back doors of the plane first, and I followed behind. He looked back as usual and blew me the last kiss of the holiday. I caught it as usual and placed it on my chest, on my heart. I probably got the wrong side where my heart actually is, but he knew what I meant. As we walked down the rickety metal stairs, the freezing cold wind of Manchester blasted into our faces. Thankfully, I had brought a cardigan for landing back in dreary old England.

It was a short walk to the terminal building, and it felt so cold. It probably wasn't even that cold, but considering what I'd been used to, it was to be expected. I was a bit annoyed too, as I looked at my tan. I didn't look as brown as I thought I was, and I had already started to peel.

I'd caught up with Sharon, and Steven had joined the rest of his friends. As we entered the terminal building and went through passport control, we were guided to the far luggage collection belt. Steven and I had already planned to go to opposite ends of the carousel so that we could minimise any potential standoffs between Ryan and Sharon. It was weird because every time I looked over at Steven, I caught Ryan looking over, the cheek of him. But this happened more than once. Piss off I thought you've got a cheek, you've missed your chance with Sharon now, even though deep down she would probably go back there in a heartbeat.

I was dying for a ciggy, but I couldn't smoke until outside the terminal building, but I got one ready in my pocket with my Crete lighter, along with another 400 Silk Cut in my case. It was about 15 minutes before the carousel started moving and the suitcases started to appear. It was as if by magic, mine was one of the first, just after the prams and beach umbrellas. I could not believe my eyes. This had never happened. Sharon followed shortly after, and we placed them on the trolley and made our way through customs. Before I started making my way, I glanced over at Steven, who was still waiting for his case. I caught his eye, and he blew me a kiss, and I blew one back for a change, and he caught it. He told me to speak tomorrow. Well, that's what I thought he said. Weirdly, I also caught Ryan's eye, too, and he waved to me and smiled. It was a nice smile and looked quite sincere. Very strange. I didn't wave back.

I don't know what it is about customs, but I always panic that I am going to be pulled aside. All I had was 400 silk cut and two bottles of ouzo, one for me and one for my Mum and Dad. We made our way through Nothing to Declare, and God knows why I was worried, as there wasn't even anyone there. I hadn't even paid attention to the customs limits. Loads of people I knew brought loads of cigarettes back from holiday and sold them in Labellos for half the price you paid for them in the shops.

Mum was waiting for us as we walked into the main area. Damn I didn't even have time for a crafty fag before I met her. I think Mum knew I smoked as she had found matches in my pocket and had smelled cigarettes on me, but I always blamed someone else.

Mum greeted me with a massive hug and I let out a massive Owww as she scraped my sunburn with her watch. She proceeded to admire my tan and start with the 100 questions that I was half prepared for.

Mum had parked in the short-stay car park about a 5-minute walk away. She started rabbiting on the fact that the cats had missed me and that I had a few letters waiting for me. She then started moaning that I hadn't rang her enough, and she was worried and disappointed I had not sent a postcard. I had no energy to reply regarding the postcard and I knew sods law it would probably arrive in the morning. All I wanted now was my bed, cuddle my cats and wait for tomorrow to arrive so I could speak to Steven.

Chapter 27

AS SOON AS I got in, I fell into bed. I couldn't help thinking how glad I was that I hadn't booked a coach holiday with Amberline like my other mates had, I'd still be in bloody Dover if I had been dribbling on the shoulder of the person sitting next to me, who probably stunk of BO. Why couldn't every man smell of Fahrenheit or Kouros like Steven?

I opened my case to get a few toiletries, a toothbrush, a flannel for a face wash and some deodorant and gave my mum and dad their ouzo. And that was it the case was left wide open full of what looked like charity shop shite and I fell into my lovely bed. My mum had put fresh bedding on and the feeling of the crisp clean quilt on my body and the feeling of a slight chill instead of a sweaty mess was the best feeling ever, well apart from lying next to Steven with his arms around me kissing my neck as we fell asleep in each other's arms.

I loved my bedroom. I had quite a big room with a double bed. And the best thing was that I had my phone in my room beside my bed. It was a round touch-tone phone, and when it rang, it had a blue neon light. Also, it meant I had privacy for my phone conversations without having to sit on the bottom stair in the hall next to the phone table any more. As cool and liberal as my parents were, a girl still needed her privacy.

I had white wallpaper with red hearts on, a poster of Patrick Swayze, and another poster from Athena of a man with no top on holding a baby, which was my favourite; he was well fit. I had typical B&Q fitted overhead wardrobes with two massive hanging wardrobes. I needed them because I was obsessed with clothes, especially since I had started working in Labellos and the fashion-conscious work colleagues and customers that came in, and I had struck up great friendships with.

There was a small area of designer clothes shops near Labellos that, at first, when I started working there, brought a tear to my eye when I saw the cost of a John Richmond top or a Westwood corset. But as time went on, I became friends with the owners, and they offered me a 20% discount on my purchases, and I realised, or maybe I was conditioned to wear these expensive items of clothing, as it made me feel better and special in a weird way. Also, considering I was only 18, I was earning good money. The hourly rate was above average, but the main thing that topped my money up was the tips when I was working behind the bar.

As I have said before Labellos was one of its kind, you could probably call it a trailblazer in the hospitality industry. The fact that it was original it attracted people with money, local business people, people who wanted to be seen with people with money and well you know the type I mean. Therefore, the tips that you would get behind the bar were off the scale. Basically, I could live off my tips through the week and save my wages for designer clothes (with discount obviously) and nights out.

Before I knew it the sun started shining through my shit curtains and woke me up. I couldn't help but wishing I was waking up with another pair of shit curtains and the heat of the Grecian sun on my face. I looked at my watch, and it had just gone 9am. I had gone totally unconscious last night, but still woke up feeling drowsy and for one minute forgot that I was back home. The first thing that came into my mind was Steven. He was calling me later, and I couldn't wait to speak to him. I know it wasn't even 24 hours since I had last spoken to him, but it felt like a lifetime. The usual worries started flicking through my mind. You know the ones, the ones that girls always worried about. I know I had slept with him, but it wasn't like a pump and dump kind of thing. It meant something, and I wasn't an idiot. I knew the feeling when I was being used. Steven was different, well, he made me feel like I wasn't a notch on his bedpost. I had to wait 9 hours until he called, and it could not come quick enough.

I was meant to be at work later today, but I seriously could not be bothered. Even though I had had a good sleep, I still felt shattered. I just needed one more day to myself, and if I admitted to myself I couldn't relax until I'd spoken to Steven. I was positive that once he had called me later, I would feel so much better, so I phoned work and said the flight was delayed for hours and I hadn't been home long. The manager was cool about it, and he said he didn't even think I was on shift anyway.

Chapter 28

I FELT PHYSICALLY sick. It was now 9pm and Steven had not rung me. I had sat next to the phone practically all day. I was like a psychopath when my mum went to call her friend earlier on, even though it was two hours before Steven had planned to call me. I kept picking the receiver up, checking for the dialling tone, making sure that the phone was still connected to BT, and that, for some unforeseen circumstances, the phone lines had gone down, but nope. Every time I picked the phone up, I was greeted with the healthy sound of the dialling tone.

I tried to stay positive. Maybe he had fallen asleep. After all he was in work today so I could understand it if he was exhausted because I was and I hadn't even been to work. After all he worked for the family business so he definitely couldn't pull a sicky.

Steven had given me his phone number so I decided to call it around 9.15pm. I was worried, this was weird and not what I expected. As I rang his number my fingers were shaking and I felt physically sick. My gut instinct was telling me something was wrong but my heart and head were telling my gut to shut up!

I rang the code for Blackpool 01253, followed by Stevens' number. I was greeted with a long tone. It was not the tone that the line was engaged in, but a tone that the number I had rung didn't exist. I double checked, well, treble checked the number Steven had given me, but I had definitely rung the correct number. I felt sick; all I could think of was to phone Sharon and tell her what had happened. Hopefully, she would make me feel better and stop me from worrying.

I rang Sharon's number and her mum answered. "Hi Nicky" you ok love, can't wait to see your holiday photos" she said. Jesus I thought I'd have to doctor the photos before anyone saw them just in case there were any inappropriate ones!

"Oh yes I'm going to take them to Max Spielman tomorrow" I told her. The line went silent and Sharon came to the phone. Sharon started babbling on about how tired she was and that she was peeling loads etc. I had to cut her short and told her that Steven hadn't called. As I expected Sharon made me feel so much better relaying to me how much he liked me and he wasn't like that bastard friend of his and there must be a reasonable excuse. Yes I thought there must be.

By this time, it was going on for 10.30pm, and I was working a long shift in the morning. I was still tired, physically and emotionally. I got into bed, and my mind was racing, but before long, I was gone.

I was at work on a 9am to 5 pm shift. I got up to the dreaded sound of my alarm clock at 7.30, took a quick shower, and washed my hair. I wasn't a high-maintenance girl; it only took me half an hour to get ready, from shower to hair drying, with minimal make-up. Bronzer, mascara, lipstick, and a squirt of Anais Anais that Steven bought me. Every time I smelled it, I thought of him. I had woken up to my stomach sinking, and I felt sick thinking about Steven. At this point, I could not even

The Wonder Bra Years

stay positive; I was filled with dread and felt so sick I couldn't even contemplate any breakfast. I'll get something later at work, I thought to myself.

I walked up for the bus and sods law it was pissing down with rain and it was windy so it was blowing my umbrella inside out. This is just what I needed this morning. As I got near the bus stop, I saw the bus coming, so I had to run for the last minute. I was so out of breath when I got to the bus stop that it looked like I needed resuscitation. I paid my fare and made my way upstairs on the bus. I got a seat near the back, settled myself, and immediately lit a cigarette. I was so stressed and worried about Steven that this cigarette would be the first of many today. Good job, I'd brought loads back with me. I must have chain-smoked the whole journey.

I got to work a bit earlier than 9.00 am, and the manager was already there. I walked in and he greeted me and asked the usual "how was your Holiday" shit. "Great," I said, didn't want to go into too much detail as at this particular moment I didn't want to explain anything because basically I didn't know myself what was happening. He gave me bits of gossip from the last two weeks. So and so had slept with so and so, etc. I was usually intrigued by this but today I couldn't give a shit.

The whole day was a bit of a blur. I set the bar up, and we opened at 12pm. It was a busy day, which was good as it took my mind off things most of the time. I'd popped out on my break to Max Spielman and put the holiday photo films in to be developed. I had 4 films and two disposable cameras to develop. God knows what was on them. I just wanted to see the pictures of Steven and me, as I was feeling quite sad. I wanted to see our happy, falling-in-love faces to see if they made me feel better. They would be ready in four days. It was a long wait, I thought, but hey, ho. When my shift finished at 5pm, a couple of the customers I was friends with asked me to have a drink with them, so I decided I'd have a few because I didn't really want to go home and be staring at the phone again all night, willing it to ring.

Cut a long story short, I got absolutely hammered because I hadn't eaten all day apart from a few chips that I had pinched off someone's food order. I ended up getting a taxi home at about 8.30pm. I had drunk red wine, then had a few Long Island Iced Teas, which were guaranteed to send me loopy. The more drunk I got the cockier I found my thoughts were thinking about Steven and it was his loss and plenty more fish in the Mersey.

I stumbled out of the taxi outside my house, paid the driver, and started fishing through my handbag, which could only be described as a Tardis because it had all kinds of things in it, and I could never find anything. I couldn't find my keys, so I had to ring the doorbell. My Dad answered the door and I practically fell inside the house. He gave me a look and a tut and left me to pick up the contents of my handbag that had emptied itself all over the hall floor, including sanitary towels and bits of chewing gum stuck to tissues and my contraceptive pill! Hope Dad hadn't seen that, I thought. I stumbled into the living room to see my mum and asked her if there had been any phone calls. She looked me up and down, shook her head and said, "Er yes." My heart stopped and I felt like life was standing still. Had he? "Sharon called about an hour ago," my mum informed me. Well, you can only imagine how that made me feel. Like shit again.

Suddenly I got a massive shot of confidence as I was pissed and decided I would call Steven again. I got the number out of my bedside drawer, as I had the night before, and proceeded to call the number. Deja vu as I got the same dead tone on the phone. What the hell! I thought. Right, my next plan of attack was to phone the directory enquiries. I rang the number, and then I froze. I did not even know Steven's bloody surname!! Oh my god, I couldn't actually believe it.

Chapter 29

I STARTED WITH my usual trying to remember something routine in my head. I would go through the alphabet hoping that when a particular letter was reached it would jog my memory. I kept going through conversations I had with Steven trying to remember if the subject of surnames ever cropped up in our conversation like the name of the family business or just general chit chat. OK I know most of the time I was pissed as a fart but I was almost sure that we had told each other this very important piece of information. Especially now when I had to be Inspector Morse and do my best detective work. But no, not a single piece of information came into my memory.

So that was it, I was absolutely buggered and had no hope of finding his number, that was if he wasn't ex-directory, I hadn't even thought of that!

It was nearly 10.00 and I was practically falling asleep. I wasn't in work the next day until 5pm, so I was thrilled at the fact I had a lie-in, that's if I could sleep. I'd grabbed a sausage roll from the fridge and some Bourbon biscuits from the kitchen cupboard and took myself off to bed. I was so sad; I think I was in shock. I could understand if this was Sharon waiting for Ryan to call her, but not my Steven. I honestly thought we had something, obviously not. It seemed all men were the same after all. I cleaned my teeth, washed my face, and took myself off to my bed. I was lying there for what seemed like ages. I had a sly ciggy out of my bedroom window and then lay on the bed. Before long, I was asleep. However, I did wake up in the middle of the night and started thinking about him again.

I woke up quite early and for one moment felt great then my stomach sank, and I remembered my situation again. Well, I thought to myself I had to get over it. He obviously wasn't bothered and to him it was probably just a stereotypical holiday romance, but to me it was more. I had to toughen up I thought, as much as I was hurting, I had to pull myself together but it was going to be tough. I had fallen in love big time.

I decided to have a lazy day before work later and tackle the pile of holiday washing I had, I did my own washing because knowing my Mum she would put my Moschino t shirt on a hot wash, and it would come out fitting a small child. I wasn't bothered when my clothes were from Miss Selfridge or the market but now Id started spending decent money on my outfits there was no way I was letting my mother near them. She was probably secretly relieved.

I was shattered after all my chores and the emotional torment I was going through so I decided to have a siesta before work. I tried to sleep but my suntan was peeling and I felt so itchy. I put loads of after sun on and felt a bit better. I dozed off for about an hour or so and then jumped in the shower to get ready for work.

I got out of the shower and I heard the phone ring. I didn't bat an eyelid as no-one rang me at this time of day. My Mum was out shopping and my dad was at work so I answered the phone in my bedroom with a quick hello because I was in a rush. As I picked up the receiver I heard pips and then the sound of a connection.

"Nicky" is that you, it's me Steven!"

I felt physically sick.

"I'm so sorry," he started. "My mum's phone is broken, and I've been on the wall at work. This is the first chance I've had."

What a load of shit I thought. It had been two days, and he could have rung before now. My initial thought was to tell him to piss off but it was my Steven and I loved him.

"I'm on my way to work," I told him. "I can't talk now."

I had a go at him even though I was so happy he had called.

"OK, I'm sorry," he replied, "I'll call you back tomorrow, I love you, and once again, I'm sorry."

It was so nice to hear his voice, but my head was all over the place. He didn't sound like he was lying, but who knows? He could be telling the truth because he had seemed so loyal and loving in Malia. I placed the phone back on the stand and sat on my bed, just sat there in a daze, almost in a trance. After a few moments, I got myself together and got ready for work, but I couldn't stop thinking about him.

The walk to the bus stop and the bus journey into town was a blur, all I could think of was Steven and what he had said about the phone being cut off etc. I decided to ring Sharon when I got to work from the manager's office phone and see what she thought, she would tell me straight!

Chapter 30

"HE'S A LYING bastard" was Sharon's thoughts on the events of earlier. Sharon was never one to mince her words. "It's taken him two days to find a phone box to call you. Something is fishy." Sharon relayed to me in quite a shouty manner. I couldn't help but agree with her. Why hadn't he called me before now? There was something not right.

I finished the call to Sharon and went back to work. It was manic. There was a stag do from Newcastle and they were a dead good laugh. I hardly had time to think about Steven. Plus, the fact that they had really sexy accents, and I noticed one of them looking over at me all the time. Still got it, I thought! He was tall, well-built and blond! I didn't usually go for blonds apart from simple Sean with the tongue. They were on the cocktails, then tequila slammers; we ran out of lemon slices in the end. They were dead funny and it made the time fly.

As the stag do was leaving, the lad who had been looking over at me passed me his number on a piece of till roll that one of the other bar staff had given him. He passed me the paper and asked me to call him at his hotel in a cheeky Geordie voice. He also told me they were going to a club called The Hippodrome and asked me to meet him there later. I knew this place as I'd been there on numerous occasions. My mate, with whom I worked, Claire, came over to me as the lads left and gave me a nudge.

"You're in there," she winked. I laughed at her response.

"They've asked me to meet them after work," I told her," fancy it?"

"Bloody right I do," she answered," they were well fit."

What was I thinking? I was in love with Steven. She had had her eye on another boy in the group, luckily, so she persuaded me to go. I hadn't told anyone about Steven yet, so I had no reason not to go as far as she was concerned. So, the plan started. Start tidying the bar and tables as much as we can so that we can finish as soon as possible. Luckily, after they had left, Labellos went strangely quiet, so the manager told us we could close half an hour early.

We had lockers in the staff changing room downstairs, and I always had a spare top and shoes in there just in case I went out after work, which seemed to be happening more and more lately.

My Tardis handbag had various bits of makeup and my Anais Anais so I had a quick armpit and vagina wash with baby wipes, topped up my make up and took my shirt and tie off and put on a black fitted bodysuit and left my black work trousers on. Claire didn't have the luxury of getting changed, so she just took her tie off and undid a few buttons on her white shirt. As we finished cleaning the bar, we sneaked a few tequila slammers ourselves, minus the lemon, so we felt a bit drunk already. It was customary to have a drink after work, so we just had another shot and raced off to The Hippodrome in a taxi.

As we worked in Labellos, which had a good reputation as a trendy bar, we only had to mention we were staff there, and we always got free admission to clubs and were escorted to the front of any queues. As we walked into the club, I had a moment of realisation. "What the hell was I doing?" I thought. Talk about a rebound, I didn't even know this lad's name. Claire and I went to the bar and ordered two double vodkas and an orange, my new drink. By this time, it was just gone 11.30pm, and it was happy hour till 12pm, so it was buy one, get one free. We didn't realise this until the bar staff brought 4 drinks over to us.

"These are with compliments from the lad at the end of the bar," the girl told me, and she nodded to the left. It was a Geordie boy, he smiled, winked and started walking over to us.

"Nice to see you Pet" he said and kissed me on the cheek, I pulled away in shock and he immediately apologised. "Sorry" he said. I didn't know how to react so my defence mechanism just pulled away.

His name was Joe. He was on his best mate's stag do and he was the best man. He was smartly dressed and smelled divine, Fahrenheit if I wasn't mistaken, my favourite smell on a man. He seemed relatively sober compared to the stag and some of the other lads in their party. Before long, some of his friends had joined us, and another round of drinks was ordered before the midnight cut-off. We had a laugh, even though it was hard to understand their accent at times.

We were chatting practically all night and Claire wandered off as she had started chatting to one of the customers that she had a crush on that came into Labellos.

Ain't Nobody by Chaka Khan came on, and Joe dragged me onto the dance floor. We had a brilliant time dancing and flirting with each other, and every time he spoke to me with the sexy Geordie accent, I felt a bit giddy! He had leaned in to kiss me a few times, but I turned my head in the nick of time. Before long, the lights came on, and it was time to go. At this point, I was starving, and luckily so was Joe, and he suggested we go for Chinese. I loved going for a Chinese meal in Chinatown. More often than not, my friends and I only went there to get an extra hour out and wait for the taxi queue to go down, but I was partial to Sui mai and prawn toast.

The club wasn't far from Chinatown, so as Joe and I started to make our way to the exit, I looked for Claire, who was nowhere to be seen. Claire was known in Labellos as a wild one, and she had no problem in sewing her wild oats if that's the saying. Joe had already spoken to his mates about us going for a Chinese, so we made our way out into the cool air to make the ten-minute walk to Chinatown.

As we were walking I linked his arm as I felt comfortable with him and I was pissed so I was probably talking all kinds of rubbish and he kept me upright. He asked me if I had a boyfriend and as I was drunk I gave him the whole story about Steven and I and the holiday romance of the century.

I was emotional but I refused to cry. I told him everything and all about the phone call situation etc. He seemed to be genuinely interested. We arrived at the Siam Garden, a lovely

Chinese restaurant that I had been to before. We walked in and Joe asked for a table for two.

We were escorted to a table near the back, and we sat down. I was starving at this point and shattered from being at work and the copious amounts of vodka. The waitress came over and Joe ordered another Vodka and orange, as well as a pint of lager for himself. He had a lovely voice. I did like the Geordie accent; it was very soothing and calm but maybe that was Joe himself that was soothing or I was pissed as a fart and on the total rebound. I can't even remember what we talked about at this point, but I do remember eating spring rolls, sui mai and prawn toast with sweet chilli and soy sauce. Best food to get when you are pissed I thought apart from my usual Curry rice and chips in a plastic container from the chippy at the top of my road.

Chapter 31

I WOKE UP the next morning and realised I was in a hotel room naked, lying next to Joe!! I felt awful. My mouth was dry, and I was self-conscious that I had no clothes on!! I usually left my wonder bra on as I was so paranoid about my small boobs but on this occasion I mustn't have cared or probably far too drunk to care.

I tried to move out of the bed like a commando on a mission, trying not to disturb or wake the half-dead, death-breath person I was in bed with. As I attempted to start my manoeuvre, I noticed one of the pads from my bra on the floor and an empty condom wrapper!!! Oh my god, I had no recollection at all from leaving the restaurant. I did not even know what hotel I was in! My trousers were on the other side of the room, and my bra and knickers were on the side of the bed on the floor.

As I stood up, I could tell I'd had sex, you know, the feeling down below! I managed to get my knickers, bodysuit and trousers on and stuffed my bra into my handbag, which was also launched onto the floor with half the contents on the carpet. I didn't know whether to wake Joe up or just sneak out. I decided to just make a run for it. I grabbed my shoes in my other hand and crept towards the door. Luckily, it looked like a nice hotel, so no creaky floors.

And the door handle opened quietly and smoothly. I closed the door behind me and ran down the corridor towards the exit sign. I realised where I was, The Moat house, the bloody Moat House. This was where Steven and I had suggested coming to. At least I had experienced this place, even though I could not remember a single thing about last night. I glanced at myself in a mirror in the hallway as I waited for the lift and I looked like boiled shite. I put mascara all around my eyes so I looked like a panda and stained my lips red. I wiped under my eyes with my finger and tried to scrub my lips. My chin was red raw again, bloody stubble rash again. Sudocrem to the rescue. This seemed to be a regular occurrence nowadays.

I walked towards the revolving doors of the entrance of the hotel, and luckily, there were a few black cabs outside at the taxi rank. I got in the first one, sat down and told the driver where I wanted to go.

What the hell had I done? I felt sick. Bacardi usually always gets me in trouble, but Vodka! This was the devil's drink. I had an awful headache, and I felt awful in more ways than one.

The journey home in the taxi was a blur. I was trying to remember things from last night. I remember the Chinese and the food, but after that, absolutely nothing. I was back at work at 1pm I looked at my watch; it was only 8.30am, so I had time for a little sleep at least. I got out of the taxi at the top of my road to go to the local corner shop. I got a can of orangeade, a pack of paracetamol, and a 10p mix (still a kid at heart). I loved the white mice and pink foamy shrimps!

I walked down my road towards my house. It was only a short walk, but I wanted to have a cigarette before I got home. I lit it up, had one puff, then threw it into the next drain as it made me feel dizzy.

I searched for my front door keys, déjà vu from the other night, but my heart sank. They were nowhere to be found. Shit they had probably fallen out of my bag in the hotel room.

I rang the doorbell and my mum answered. "Where have you been" she enquired? I couldn't possibly tell her Id had a one-night stand with a man from Newcastle and stayed the night in a hotel with him and that I didn't remember a single thing could I?

"Oh, I stayed in Claire's," I replied sheepishly. Mum then started telling me that I had missed three phone calls from a gentleman called Steven. Well, if I'd felt sick earlier, I would feel even worse now. I felt like I had cheated on him. Had I? I was by no means an expert in the art of dating and relationships, but I assumed having sex with someone other than the person you're supposed to love was technically cheating. "He's going to call back today, "Mum said. "Oh, and I'm not your bloody secretary, Nicky," as she walked away towards the garden, stomping her slippers on the floor.

All I wanted to do at this moment was get a shower, and I felt dirty and smelled of cigarettes and stale perfume. I jumped in the shower, threw my clothes in the dirty washing basket, scrubbed myself clean, and washed my hair. I just stood under the warm water for about five minutes thinking about last night, and my stomach churned when I thought of everything, I mean I hadn't murdered anyone but I still felt like crap. I decided to wet my hair again later and blow-dry it for work. I had no energy now; all I wanted was my bed. As I walked into my room my quilt had no cover on, bloody mother had washed my bedding. Sod it I thought and climbed under the bare quilt which felt slightly uncomfortable and itchy on my peeling skin but I didn't care. I set my alarm for 11am just in case and drifted off, I'd already had a shower and I thought to myself I'd get a taxi into work as I was shattered.

I was woken up harshly by my mum shouting up the stairs that I had a phone call. What I thought! I had not heard a single thing, even though I had a phone right next to my bed. I reached for the receiver on my bedside table and heard the click of my mum hanging up the phone in the hall.

"Eventually your home," I heard in a jolly voice. Shit it was Steven. I did a sort of staged laugh pretending that everything was hunky dory. I had no energy to speak properly, but Steven sounded elated and on top of the world. "Guess what babe" he started, I'm coming to see you later and I've booked us a room at the Moat House, I'll be there for 7pm for when you finish work so meet me there, See I remembered the name of the place you told me."

Oh My God I thought, The bloody Moat House. Of all the hotels in all of Liverpool he picked this one.

Shit, I thought, Joe and his mates were staying at the Moat House another night. This wasn't happening to me, surely. Fifty out of fifty-two weeks of the year, I had no action at all, and suddenly in one bloody weekend, I had two fellas on the go and both staying in the same place.

I remembered that Steven and I had discussed staying at The Moat House as it was the hotel where my gym was situated so I know that's why he had booked here. I tried to go to the gym three times a week and have a workout and a swim but lately it had been more like three times a month. I know he had booked this to be romantic and thoughtful after letting me down again but all I could think of was bumping into Joe who I had sex with last night.

Well, I was assuming I had. What the hell was I going to do?

Chapter 32

AS I HUNG up the phone to Steven, I froze on the edge of my bed for the second day on the run. Basically, I had to get my bits together for a night of passion in a hotel with my holiday romance true love, nice clothes, underwear, shave armpits, legs, and cultivate a bikini line and pray that I didn't bump into the fella I'd been with the night before in the same place. I proceeded with the tasks required and grabbed my head bag and placed a nice black dress, my Wolford tights, Wonderbra, stilettos and my toiletries bag that I hadn't unpacked yet from Malia. Well, I hadn't had any time, had I? I'd been too busy being constantly drunk or waking up with strange men. I had already started to re do my hair and put the straighteners on it and sprayed a bit of Insette and packed the can in my bag along with fresh knickers and Anais Anais.

By this time, it was gone 12.20, so I rang the local taxi firm and booked my taxi into town. I told my mum I was staying at Claire's again after work. I gave her some bullshit that her Grandad was sick and she was upset etc. I know I have said my mum was cool, but I definitely think she would have something to say about all this. Bloody hell I'm going to end up in one of my mum's crappy magazines at this rate. You literally could not make this up.

I should have been looking forward and feeling excited to seeing Steven later but all I could think of was bumping into

Joe at the hotel. How the hell did I get myself into such situations? It must be the Vodka.

The taxi arrived and it was the usual weirdo driver that wore leather gloves!! He seemed pleasant enough but the gloves always made me shudder! The traffic was quiet so it didn't take long to get to town. He never made any small talk, he just looked into his mirror constantly, looked at me and smiled. Creepy.

I walked into work, slightly apprehensive and still shattered from last night. As I always did when I arrived at work I said hello to the girls/lads on shift and walked downstairs to the staff changing area and lockers so I could hang my clothes up and put my bits in my locker.

Before I could go downstairs Paul who was on shift shouted me. "Eh You" some Geordie lad has been in looking for you and left you this" Oh god what I thought. Surely it couldn't get any worse.

Paul handed me a note and a set of house keys. I opened the white piece of paper slowly and nervously. It read "I had a lovely night, gutted you weren't there when I woke up, hopefully see you later, my room number is 112 in case you don't remember" J and two kisses!

Well, if I wasn't panicking before, I certainly was now.

Now let's get this situation into perspective, I thought to myself. The love of my life had booked a room in a lovely hotel for us this evening to experience a sensual, loving evening. And while all this is going on, I'm going to be on pins that I will

The Wonder Bra Years

bump into the boy I'd probably had sex with last night, but not remember a single part of it. At least I had told Joe about Steven, that bit I do remember.

My shift at the bar went by so slow it was as if time had stood still. I was constantly looking at the front door to see if Joe walked in with the rest of the stags but luckily they didn't. I was hoping they were all so hungover that they couldn't possibly contemplate venturing out until the evening but I kept thinking that Joe had obviously been up and about early as he had dropped my keys off with the "note."

I looked at my watch. It was 6.15 pm, and it was 45 minutes to go, until I felt like I was sort of in the clear. I looked again at 6.30, 6,40, 6.50!!! Ten minutes till safety. 7pm... I'd done it. No sign of Joe.

The staff starting at 7pm had already arrived, luckily, so as soon as the little hand hit 7, I went downstairs to the staff room and sat down on an old bar stool to get myself together.

"Right," I thought, this situation can go two ways, so let's try and stay positive and hope that I didn't end up in the middle of two men in the middle of a hotel reception area.

I had an outfit for my night out with Steven, but I had also packed an outfit that made me look like I always look this casual and gorgeous to arrive at the hotel. It was mad thinking we would see each other in England clothes and not shorts and t-shirts. I started getting ready, which didn't take me long, as I'd decided I'd take a shower at the hotel.

Then suddenly a big sudden thought came into my head! What if Steven hadn't even arrived at the hotel? When we spoke on the phone last night he told me he would leave our room number at reception. Oh god, I hope it wasn't the same receptionist as last night and this morning!! I just prayed that the gods, buddha, Allah and all gods possible that I could think of from religious studies were on my side today.

Roughly about 15 minutes later, I left work and started walking towards the hotel, which was only 5 minutes away. I was on pins the whole time, looking left and right and listening for Geordie accents. Soon enough, I was at the entrance of The Moat House, its flags flying outside, and a gentleman in a suit greeting all the visitors. I walked in towards reception and bumped into one of my mates from the gym. She started babbling on about something, but I just nodded, gave her a hug, and walked off. She probably thought I was a snotty cow, but I didn't care. As I walked towards reception, the receptionist smiled at me and said, "Hello again." I froze. Hello again, oh my god!!! I wish I had my roller boots with me just in case I needed to make a swift exit. But unfortunately, the stoppers fell off years ago. She must have been working last night or this morning, but I couldn't remember. My youth theatre acting days came into effect, and I nodded. Luckily, as I was just about to speak, I felt a tap on my shoulder.

"What time do you call this, babe?" I knew it was Steven. As I turned around, I literally fell into his arms. He was still as beautiful as I had remembered. As soon as I embraced him, I melted and could not wait to go upstairs with him and say hello properly. I totally forgot about everything else.

"Come on," he said, "Give me your bag, we are in room 119."

"119," I thought, holy shit, Room 119, 7 doors down from room 112!

Chapter 33

AS SOON AS we reached 119, we fell into the room and fell into each other's arms onto the bed. The first thing I thought was that this was a nicer room than last night. Much nicer curtains and tea and coffee facilities! My memory seemed to be coming back. Within a few minutes we were making love, just like we had in Malia. It was passionate and sensual and I felt so comfortable even though I still had my doubts after the late phone call situation.

As we finished we squeezed each other and kissed, it was amazing to be in Stevens arms again. Our moment of love and tenderness was rudely interrupted by a knock at the door.

"Who the hell was that" I thought. My body froze and immediately thought the worst. Joe? Surely not. How would he know I was here? If the receptionist had told him I would be sending a ruddy big customer service complaint in regarding lack of privacy! "Room Service" I heard.

Steven jumped up, pulled on his grey tracksuit bottoms and went to answer the door. I pulled the crisp white sheets over my body and tried to hide my face just in case it was a member of staff from last night, I was paranoid! After a few seconds I sneakily glanced up to Steven walking back towards me with a bottle of Moet Champagne in an ice bucket with two champagne flutes. I breathes a sigh of relief.

Steven always had a knack for making me laugh. He placed the ice bucket down on the table and proceeded to remove his grey sexy jogger bottoms whilst trying to dance. I felt embarrassed because I was sober, but also extremely intrigued as to what would happen next. He turned away, showing his very tight white bum cheeks, and placed a white hand towel over his forearm. He grabbed the ice bucket again and started walking towards the bed, pretending to be a waiter!

"Would madam like a glass of the finest champagne?" he said, half laughing and half Manuel from Fawlty Towers. I was crying and laughing. This was my Steven, the one who made me feel safe and had a silly sense of humour like me. Oh, I forgot to mention that he also loved Star Wars like me. I don't know how I got into Star Wars; I can probably blame my dad, but I honestly couldn't remember. Wish I could use the force to get me out of this pickle.

Time flew by, and before we knew it, it was nearly 9pm. "Right, where are you taking me tonight?" Steven said. Well, I needed a shower first. I jumped out of bed and covered myself with a towel because I was sober and was so conscious of my body, even though he had seen it all previously. I didn't have to wash my hair; I just needed to go over it with my steam straighteners or the iron in the room, as I'd done millions of times. I plugged them in before I got into the shower.

As I got into the shower Steven decided to try and join me but I threw him out in a playful manner. "Oi you that's enough shenanigans for now." He laughed and splashed me with water and got my hair wet! I was fuming! But luckily for him it was easily solved with the hairdryer in the hotel attached to the wall.

I left the water running, and Steven got in as I left and gave me a few minutes for my privacy to sort my bits and bobs out.

I couldn't help myself while he was in the shower, but I wanted to look through his bag to see if anything untoward appeared. I had roughly three minutes, so I quickly rummaged through his holdall. Nothing appeared to be out of place apart from a small bottle of Rush! I knew what this was straight away as it had been forced into my nostrils on a few occasions. I was a bit shocked but quite thankful I'd found Rush and not anything regarding another girl. I hope he didn't bring it out. I hated the smell, and it gave me a headache.

I put my Wolford shiny tights on with the seam at the back as straight as I could with my black Wonderbra and thong, and then the "piece de resistance" fitted black elasticated dress from Wade Smith. As Steven walked out of the bathroom, he stood for a second and looked at me. "Wow, Nic, you look amazing. I'm a lucky man." I got embarrassed and told him to shut up. I hated compliments and never knew how to react. He wouldn't think he was a lucky man if he knew what I'd been up to seven doors down last night.

Next minute our moment was interrupted by a noise of a gang of lads outside our room laughing and joking loudly. It must be the stags I thought. I listened closely and I could hear the Newcastle dialect. Right, I thought, I will have to do something to delay us so that we didn't bump into them in the bar downstairs, but I was dressed and ready to go so this wasn't really an option so I just hoped for the best.

I'd managed to distract Steven for a few more minutes. I pretended I was looking for something in my bag and took a while longer with my make up until it all went quiet in the hallway, it seemed to be safe now but I was now worrying that they might all be downstairs, I hoped not because it was bloody expensive as all hotel bars were and not particularly anything exciting going on apart from couples or families on a weekend break or to see the sights or Beatles fans. And as I worked in the area of The Cavern, there were always plenty of Beatles fans, even though I didn't see the attraction myself.

Steven got himself all spruced up. Chino trousers, white ben Sherman shirt (he still had a lovely suntan) and a pair of Rockport boots and he smelt amazing, Kouros if I wasn't mistaken! I felt proud to be seen out with him but I was also shitting myself about bumping into Joe.

Chapter 34

We left the hotel room holding hands. We had drunk the champagne so I felt quite drunk, probably the lack of food and my nerves. As we walked towards the lift my nerves hit an all-time high as I was panicking about bumping into the stag party in reception. Steven had suggested going to Labellos because he wanted to see where I worked but there was no way I was taking him there just in case. I told him it was the Quiz night and it was rubbish. There was never a quiz night.

The only thing I could think of was the other end of the city, Concert Square. There were loads of bars there, and it was usually good and always busy, even though it wasn't my usual haunt. As the lift door opened on the ground floor, I kept my head to my chest and into Steven's arm as much as I could. It seemed all quiet, so I think I'd dodged a bullet!

We walked towards the revolving doors and the smartly dressed gentleman greeted us and said, "have a nice evening folks." "We will" Steven replied and we walked into the evening air that was warm and soothing. Concert Square wasn't far so we walked up Hanover Street still holding hands.

We walked towards Concert Square and we went to the Arena bar. This was quite a trendy bar, usually you could bump into Liverpool FC footballers at the weekend when they had a home game.

Steven ordered me my usual Vodka and orange and he got a bottle of sol with the lime segment in the top!

I still couldn't relax, I kept looking over my shoulder for a raucous gang of Geordie stags, but so far I was safe. We had another round of drinks, and Steven suggested that we go for food. I needed some food to soak up the booze.

I wasn't a big restaurant person; I'd rather just get drunk, but I did think I would benefit from lining my stomach as I had a feeling this night would involve copious amounts of Bacardi or Vodka now.

The only place I could think of that was nice and not far was the Mexican place El Macho that I had been to with the Labellos staff on the training week. Also, I thought it might make me look sophisticated if I knew what refried beans and guacamole were even though I'd rather go to Wimpy.

It was only a short walk, I'd usually get a taxi when I was with my friends, just because my high heels would give me a blister, but it was also a lovely warm evening, so a walk didn't seem so bad. I'd totally forgotten about bumping into the stags, and I was starting to relax and enjoy my night with Steven.

We got to the restaurant and were escorted to a table for two at the back that was lit up only by candlelight and you could hear the background music ever so slightly that added to the romantic atmosphere.

Steven ordered us a bottle of wine and a glass of lemonade for me in case I did not like it, and it tasted like vinegar! Wine was a weird one with me; I didn't appreciate a good wine. I wouldn't drink red wine. I tasted it once at my aunt's, and it was disgusting. As I had hoped, Steven did not have a clue about the

Mexican menu, so I styled it out and advised him on what he should have, and I could tell he was very impressed. "Well, Nicky, you never fail to surprise me! Who would have thought you knew the difference between salsa and sour cream?" he sniggered! I couldn't tell if he was taking the piss or was genuinely impressed. Obviously, salsa is red and sour cream is white, I thought.

After looking at the menu for what seemed like a lifetime we decided on Nachos to start and we both ordered Mexican spiced chicken with rice and chips.

We made small talk and told each other about our week. Obviously, I didn't tell him the truth. I just said I'd been working loads. I was dying to ask him more about the phone number situation, but I didn't have the nerve to ask. The main thing I wanted to ask him was what his surname was. I casually enquired about this a few minutes later.

"It's Smith," he replied, "Bloody hell, girl, your memory is awful" Smith! Smith! Oh well, there must be about a million Smiths on directory enquiries, so that line of enquiry would have been out the window the other night anyway.

Our food arrived, and I hadn't realised how hungry I was. Steven commented on how fast I ate again, as he had done in Malia. "Well, I'm a growing girl," I answered back. I did like my food, and this food was spectacular, and Steven seemed to enjoy it too. The waitress collected our empty plates and asked us if we wanted dessert. I never got pudding, I would be fit for nothing; luckily, he was the same. He asked for the bill, and when it came, he paid. I offered to go halves; I was in no way serious, but I wanted to seem like I was a modern woman type thingy. He shot me down in a flash and insisted on paying. Phew, I didn't have much money on me anyway. Enough for a few drinks later, though, I thought.

"So, where you are taking me now?" Steven asked. Well, I thought to myself this was a tricky one. There were a few bars a few minutes away that I went to quite a lot.

"Plummers," I suggested, "it's always good in there."

We walked outside, turned right and we were there.

There was always a queue to get into Plumbers, but as I worked in Labellos, I was always guaranteed to get in straight away and not have to wait in a queue. I knew a few of the doormen, so as soon as they saw me, they gestured to me to just walk in. Steven glanced at me as if to say, "State of you," but this was commonplace to me. I'm sure that's why my friends loved me. In front of any queue at any bar and even free entrance into nightclubs, I just had to buy the doorman a drink to keep him sweet.

Plumbers was busy, and they were playing brilliant music, like old soul and funk stuff, the type that makes you want to dance when you are drunk. We were chatting, dancing and kissing. I saw loads of people I knew. They came up to me and gave me a double kiss. I had to introduce Steven to a few people, especially as soon as he spoke, they realised he wasn't from around here. As we were both drunk, we told everyone how we had met on holiday, etc. There were a few raised eyebrows when we mentioned the Holiday romance cliché, but mostly people seemed happy for us and wished us luck. We were probably annoying people around us as we looked like a smug couple in love. It was amazing, and this was what I had envisaged we would be like when we came back from Greece.

Every now and again I shit myself when a lively gang of lads seemed to arrive, alerting me to the Joe situation. I had either been lucky not to bump into them or it was the calm before the storm.

Steven and I suddenly seemed quite drunk and frisky so decided to head back to the hotel. Fingers and everything crossed that it would be a seamless transition from this bar to our hotel room!

Chapter 35

WE HAD A brilliant walk back to The Moat House. We were both drunk but not wanting to vomit drunk. Just happy and giggly drunk. On the walk back, there was a street busker singing American Pie. I don't know how this happened, but I knew most of the words to this song. So, as I was drunk, I decided to start singing with him. Steven was standing there laughing and clapping along with me, and then he pulled me away when it came to a point when I struggled to remember the words! My parents had an eclectic taste in music, ranging from Status Quo to The Eagles to Pink Floyd, so unusually, I knew all kinds of songs that a normal teenager wouldn't.

The final few minutes' walk towards the hotel we stumbled and laughed the entire journey there. The well-suited gentleman was still on the door and greeted us with his usual well- mannered greeting.

The hotel bar seemed lively and busy at first glance. "Shall we have a nightcap before we go up?" Steven suggested. My reply was delayed as I scoured the bar area looking for Joe or any sign of a Newcastle accent. I was so drunk, but I couldn't see anything immediately, so I had a burst of confidence and agreed. I was desperate for a wee, so I told Steven I was going to the toilet while he went to the bar. I walked away towards the ladies and bumped right into Joe!! His face lit up with delight, and mine looked like I had seen a ghost.

"Oh, Nicky, I can't believe you've come to see me, Pet! You've made my night," Joe proceeded to babble and put his arms around me! What the hell was I going to say? I needed to come up with something quickly, or tell him the truth. I decided to be honest, it wasn't fair to Joe, and after all, I'd only met him once, not like Steven and me, who had a connection. But I had to be quick as Steven was waiting for me in the bar.

"Hold on here a second," I told Joe, "I just need to sort something with my mate."

Joe stood there quietly as I walked off towards the bar of the hotel to join Steven and try and think of an excuse so that I could disappear for 10 minutes to explain everything to Joe but Steven was nowhere to be seen.

I looked all over the bar area and then the bar maid asked me if my name was Nicky. "Yes it is," I answered totally paranoid. She told Mr Smith had taken our drinks upstairs and to meet him up there. Thank god.

Right, I had to decide what to do and quick sharp!! I wanted to explain to Joe the situation, but I also wanted sexy time with Steven. I decided on the sexy time. I rushed up to our room, fixed my boobs into as good a position as possible with what I had to work with and entered our room to an unconscious snoring open legged man lying flat out on the bed! I walked towards him and gave him a nudge! Not a single movement! No action there for a good few hours I thought.

I had two choices in front of me. Try and wake Steven up or sneak back downstairs to see Joe. Steven was well away so I thought he won't miss me for half an hour so. And I did feel guilty about Joe and I felt like I needed to give him an explanation.

I went into the bathroom quietly and sprayed deodorant and checked my face, mascara and lipstick touch up with a spray of Anais Anais and I was on my way out of the room as quiet as a mouse and made my way back downstairs, I double checked Steven was still asleep first, which he was and I was off.

I arrived back at the hotel bar, and Joe, God love him, was still waiting for me.

Chapter 36

I WALKED TOWARDS Joe full of nerves and slight excitement and guilt. God knows why because I was about to tell him I was staying 7 doors down from him with my holiday romance boy. I did explain everything to Joe about Steven the night I met him but whether he had remembered or just humoured me so he could sleep with me that night I'll never know.

He had sat down in the bar area, and God loved him. He got me a Vodka. Not another. Half of me was touched that he remembered, but the other half of me thought the worst, another drunken night. He stood up as I walked towards him and pulled a chair out, chivalry at its finest. This made me think of Steven on our last night on holiday in the Italian restaurant. As I sat down, he pulled my chair towards the table. I grabbed my drink and had a massive swig, not very ladylike, but I needed the courage.

Joe started going on about how thrilled he was to see me, but I had to cut him short as I felt like a fake and wanted to tell him the truth. I started telling him what had happened after I left him that morning. It was hard to tell him the truth as I could tell he did genuinely like me, and it broke my heart that someone so nice was interested in me as a person and not just for you know what. Joe sat there quietly as I explained everything. He didn't say anything at first, and I could swear I could see a tear in his eye. This was hard to do because I did like him, and if Steven wasn't in the picture, I would be delighted to have met someone as lovely as him.

Joe then made my decision for me as he stood up to walk away. "Thanks for being honest, Nicky, he said, "But I'm not being second best to anyone. I hope it works out, and I won't cause any issues while I'm in the hotel, OK?" He kissed my cheek, looked into my eyes, turned his back and walked away! I felt sick. Deflated and sad, but what else could I do? He was so lovely, but I loved Steven. I sat there for a few minutes, finished my drink in one. I was a bit shocked by his reaction, considering we had only met once, but sometimes when you meet someone, you just click, and you can't help your feelings, I suppose. It had happened to me loads of times, and I always ended up the one getting hurt. I respected his decision, and I felt bloody awful.

I made my way to the lifts to go back to Steven, surely he will be awake by now wondering where I am. As I walked towards our room I could hear loud voices. As I got to the door it was Steven's raised voice I could hear on the hotel room phone. I pressed my ear to the door before I opened it to try and listen to the conversation. I couldn't quite make out exactly what was said and half of me didn't want to.

I forced my way into the room quickly so I would catch him mid phone conversation and Steven slammed the phone down immediately.

"Who was that?" I shouted. Steven stared at me with a startled face.

"No one," he answered.

"Liar," I shouted. "I heard everything."

I hadn't heard anything at all apart from shouting but I wasn't going to let him know that. He stood up and stated pacing the floor.

"Nicky, it was nothing," he started, "it was just my mum asking what time I would be home tomorrow"

I knew he was lying; I could tell by his face. I stormed towards the wardrobe and started packing my things into my headbag. He grabbed my arm and turned me towards him.

"Nicky," "I swear it's nothing to be upset about."

Yet again, my head was telling me to leave, but my heart wanted me to stay and cuddle him and make love all night. I looked at my watch and it was gone 2am, and I couldn't be bothered making my way home now, plus the fact that I was very drunk. Probably too drunk to make any rational decisions. One thing I will say about Steven is his ability to win me over with his charm and his obvious good looks. But I knew something was not right.

"Something isn't right," I started. I don't believe you, but I want to!"

I started my full-on essay on all my doubts, starting with him not calling me for two days, his phone number not connecting, and him calling me from a pay phone! He told me yet again about his mum's phone not working and not having time to call. That was one point I definitely did not believe. "There are hundreds of pay phones, but it took you two days," I shouted! Didn't you have any ten-pence coins?" At this point, I

The Wonder Bra Years

was conscious of the volume of my voice, and I didn't want the hotel to throw us out.

"I know there are but I didn't have your number with me," he cried. I could tell he was upset "Your number was in mine in the drawer by my bed, I didn't take it to work with me! Sorry I just didn't think" Fair enough point as his number was in my bedside drawer.

I listened to his plea, and it did seem slightly believable, or maybe I was just too tired and drunk to think more of it at this time. I was crying and upset, so I sat on the edge of the bed and put my head into my hands. Steven sat next to me and put his arm around me. I shrugged it off quite forcefully and moved away. There was no way I was sleeping with him now; I couldn't bring myself to.

On the other side of the room there was a small two-seater sofa. "Well, you can sleep on there tonight," I shouted to him. I stood up and grabbed my toiletries bag and went to the bathroom and locked the door behind me. I placed the lid of the toilet down and sat there for a few minutes just thinking about what I was going to do. I didn't want to leave the room and go home because I was pissed and shattered but then I also thought about going back downstairs to see Joe. I was feeling unloved, and I felt I needed attention. God knows what I would say to Joe, but at that moment, I decided that my next move was to find him downstairs. I cleaned my face from the black mascara tears and replaced my Lechner foundation, Arabian glow, and lipstick. Quick spray of perfume and a double-quick flannel wash of the important areas, and I unlocked the bathroom door.

Steven was sitting on the sofa, looking all forlorn and sorry for himself.

"I'm going downstairs for a drink, I saw someone I know from the gym earlier so I'm going to find her" I told him "And I don't want you to follow me," and I gave him a scornful look, such a liar but I didn't feel the remotest bit of guilt. I could not be bothered with him at the moment; he looked pathetic, and I was so angry. I walked to the hotel room door and tried to slam it behind me, but it didn't have the desired effect as it was on a slow release!

Typical! I walked towards the lift and made my way downstairs to the bar. I just hoped Joe was still there, and I did not have a clue what I was going to say to him.

At least I knew his room number if he wasn't there.

Chapter 37

THE LIFT PINGED at ground floor so I put my best foot forward and made my way to the bar area that was still quite busy. I saw some of Joes friends but I could not see Joe anywhere. I went to the bar and ordered a double Bacardi and coke and a tequila shot and got them charged to room 119. I'd had enough of Vodka and I decided I would never drink it again out of principle!

I felt awkward standing on my own, and I didn't really have the confidence to go over to the stag party even though I had met a few of them the other night. Luckily, one of them recognised me and shouted at me. Phew, I thought at least I had an intro into the group sitting around two sofas and tables. There were a few girls sitting with them, and one was sitting on the stag's knee.

I asked where Joe was and a few of the lads shrugged their shoulders and the stag pointed over to a dark area at the back of the bar. I glanced over and I saw Joe sitting with a tarty looking girl in the corner. She was probably a lovely girl but my jealous streak had made an appearance and I didn't know what to do. I felt sick to my stomach and really jealous that he looked like he had moved on so quickly.

So, I did what any normal girl would do. I did the Tequila in one and had a large swig of the Bacardi, shuddered, and started walking over to the darkened area. As I walked over Joe turned his head and looked straight at me. He looked like he had seen a ghost, like I had earlier. He stood up immediately, looking all flustered, and walked towards me, so we met sort of halfway.

"Nicky, what you are doing back down here?" He asked me. His voice was shaky and nervous. I was bloody nervous too but I tried to act cool as a cucumber even though I was dying inside with nerves.

"I felt like another drink," I mumbled "You know me, Party animal and all that." God, I sounded like a right idiot. "I can see you're busy, though, so I'll leave you to it," and I gave him a sarcastic wink and proceeded to turn my back and walk away.

"No, stay," Joe answered as he grabbed my wrist and pulled me back towards the darkened area. "Wait here," he whispered and turned towards the girl.

He went over to her, said something in her ear, and she stood up abruptly, pushing her seat away behind her. She looked me up and down and gave me a right dirty look! Oh, shit I will probably get beaten up later I thought. I hated confrontations of any form, but as I was drunk, I stood there firmly even though I was pooing my pants!

The girl walked away in her thigh-high boots, and she looked like she needed a good wash! Anyway, this was not the time or place to be a bitch, I had bigger things to worry about. Joe, ever the gentleman, pulled a chair out for me, and he sat next to me.

He grabbed his drink, A steamboat if I wasn't mistaken, I could tell by the smell of the Southern Comfort, and he had a massive gulp, practically finishing it. I could tell by his face that he was as nervous as I was.

"Why are you back down here?" Joe asked, his voice was quite shaky. "Was your fella asleep?"

I was thinking what to say, I did not know whether to tell him the truth or make a pack of lies up. I decided to be honest with him. I hadn't lied to him from the start. I decided to order us some drinks first and put the bill onto the room again. I beckoned the waitress over and ordered another double Bacardi for me and a double steamboat for Joe. Joe tried to pay but I insisted and he eventually relented. I still had some of my first drinks left, so I grabbed them, drank some, and started telling Joe what had happened. I started from when I had left Joe earlier to go back to my room. I explained I could hear Steven on the phone, but not exactly what was being said. The waitress interrupted my flow with the drinks.

"Charge to room 119," I told her, she nodded and walked away. I should order more champagne I thought but secretly I didn't even like it. I continued explaining to Joe what had happened and how I was feeling. He sat there looking into my eyes and he was listening to every word I said. There was a silent pause from both of us. I was waiting for him to reply to my story and give me his opinion. He grabbed his drink and sipped it a few times, and then he looked like he was about to start telling me what an idiot I was, etc. And lo and behold, he did, but in a nice way.

"Nicky," I don't know what to say to you! To me, he sounds like the right player, and you need to tell him where to go! You need to find out who he was talking to, but I'm not going to be here playing second fiddle to him while you make your mind up."

I totally agreed to what he had said and as I was totally pissed I started to proceed with what can only be described as the biggest heartfelt speech I had ever made.

"Joe, I agree but Steven and I have something special, something I have never experienced before, I've always been let down by men even though I'm not the most experienced girl in the world."

Joe gave me a wink and said, "I beg to differ going by the other night."

We laughed, and I wanted the ground to swallow me up with embarrassment, and this broke the ice slightly. God knows what I'd done with him in room 112! Probably best I didn't remember anything.

I continued telling him my doubts about Steven and my gut feelings about him. I was so confused. I thought it was meant to be easy when you were in love.

It was getting late and some of the lights went out in the main bar area. Seemed like it was closing time.

"Do you want to come to my room to finish our drinks?" Joe asked.

The Wonder Bra Years

I knew if I went upstairs with him I would probably get carried away again and I wasn't sure whether I wanted that, or did I?

Chapter 38

JOE PICKED UP our drinks, and I followed him towards the lifts. What the hell was I doing? I was drunk and vulnerable, but still very angry at Steven. My initial thought was just to go to his room for half an hour to finish my drink. I just prayed the bar staff got amnesia overnight before I checked out tomorrow.

As I walked into the room it looked like a bomb had gone off in it. Typical lads on tour. Clothes on floor, ashtrays overflowing and loads of empty glasses. Joe looked embarrassed and proceeded to make the bed hurriedly and clear the bedside tables of cigarette ash and half drank cans of lager.

I laughed out loud and sat on the side of the bed that looked the cleanest. I looked at my watch and it was nearly 3.30 am. Luckily I wasn't in work tomorrow but I was till shattered physically and emotionally.

Joe started throwing clothes and bits and bobs into his holdall. I knew he was going back to Newcastle tomorrow, but I had no clue what time his train was.

"What times your train tomorrow?" I enquired.

"12.30pm," he answered. " I'm going to be dead pet," he giggled and gave me a wink! He was funny and I did really fancy him, actually I fancied him loads. He was different to Steven. He was tall and blond. As I've said before I don't usually go for blonds but he was gorgeous. Think Chesney Hawkes but with better hair.

He jumped up onto the bed next to me and lay on his elbow with his head resting on his hand. God, he looked so sexy!! I am definitely going to have to pull every bit of willpower in my body to resist this situation.

"Joe, I don't know what I'm doing." I started trying my best not to start crying, but I could feel my eyes filling up. Joe wiped my tears away, moved towards me, and started kissing me. I didn't pull away; if anything, I jumped in headfirst. Before I knew it, we were kissing passionately, and we had moved down the bed, and we were lying down, and our bodies were moving closer together. The kisses were passionate, and it felt right even though I knew it wasn't. I stopped myself before things went any further. I didn't want this. I wanted Steven. I was so confused, and I didn't want to lead Joe any further, but I couldn't help myself. Well, yes, you guessed it, my Wonderbra was on the floor of room 112 yet again!

The sex was amazing, and I remembered every single bit. It was romantic and sensual, but exciting and fun at the same time. I got lost in the moment, and when we had finished, Joe hugged me so tight and kissed me on the forehead. I know this sounds so soppy, but it was truly lovely. I was waiting for him to get up and go to the bathroom or something along those lines, but he didn't. We lay there holding each other; it was just that. Holding each other tight, and I didn't want to let go.

We still had a bit of our drinks left, so Joe suggested getting room service. "What do you want?" he asked. My room this time?" He laughed.

I didn't really want any more alcohol, but I was starving and thirsty.

"Can I have a cheese and ham toastie and half a lager and lime?" I answered. "Ha-ha," he laughed so hard I thought he was going to fall off the bed. "Definitely," he said, "want some chips too?" I nodded in agreement as he placed the call to room service. "That's what I like about you, Nicky," Joe giggled. "You're like one of the lads, but I really fancy you" I sat up in shock, a bit shocked by his answer. I could tell he knew he had said the wrong thing. "No, I don't mean that in a bad way," he quickly tried to reassure! I was winding him up I thought that was a compliment, even though it didn't sound like one. We finished our original drinks and lay on the bed chatting about this and that. Joe worked for the local council in the offices, sorting out benefits, etc. He told me he had started there on a YTS scheme when he left school, but had worked his way up. I was impressed with his work ethic, and he continued to tell me about his ambitions to work his way up the company ladder.

Knock, knock, someone was at the door. For one second, I'd forgotten we had ordered room service and imagined Steven on the bounce at the door. Panic over, it was only our toasties.

Joe answered the door after quickly throwing his jeans back on. He wheeled the trolley in with two plates with silver cloches over each plate. Oo-er, I thought so posh for a toastie and chips. As usual, I ate my food in my record-breaking fashion and washed it down with the lager and lime. As soon as I had finished, it was as if someone had pulled my plug out, and I was out of energy, and I desperately needed to sleep.

"I'll have to go back to my room," I said sadly to Joe who was still only halfway through his food. He reluctantly agreed even though both of us just wanted to fall asleep together.

"Will I see you before I leave?" Joe asked as he grabbed my hand. I wanted to be realistic with him but I had Steven seven doors down and I suppose he was expecting me to see him to the train station.

"I'm leaving here just after 11.30," Joe said, "please come and see me before I leave, promise Nicky?"

"I promise," I said. And I meant it.

Chapter 39

IT WAS GONE 5.00am when I sneaked back into room 119. I opened the door, and the room was in darkness apart from the slight light coming from the bathroom. Luckily, this enabled me to see where I was going. I went to the bathroom, had a wee and cleaned my teeth and my down belows, but I couldn't be bothered washing my face. I didn't flush the toilet as I didn't want to wake Steven up. I know I'd broken the cardinal rule of washing makeup off, preventing spots, but I was too tired to care. As I left the bathroom, I grabbed a t-shirt from my bag and got into bed. Steven was in bed. Even though Id told him not too I didn't blame him as I had buggered off and left for a good few hours. As soon as I lay down, I realised I had slept with two different men in one day! I couldn't believe what was happening, but before long, I was gone, unconscious. I just hoped I woke up in time to see Joe before he went in the morning, and I didn't have long to wait.

I was woken up by Steven answering the room door to room service with two full English breakfasts under silver cloches, probably the same as last nights!! He had ordered coffee, fresh orange juice and a lovely, cooked breakfast for us both. Nice touch I thought but I was still angry and I needed time to sort my head out, plus I now had Joe in the equation.

"Shit Joe," I thought. I glanced at my watch; it was 10.45. Shit I thought what am I going to do and how can I get out of this one. I still had 45 minutes; I knew I could eat quickly, but I needed to make an excuse to leave, and I wasn't sure I wanted to. Oh god, I was so confused. I loved Steven; well, I think I did, but he made me doubt him on so many levels. I started thinking about all the letdowns. He let me down on the last day of the holiday, didn't call me for two days and then the suspicious phone call in the hotel room! The doubts were mounting up. The atmosphere between us was frosty, almost frozen. Steven was being ultra-nice, over the top in parts. A few times, I started to thaw slightly, but then I thought of Joe, and the clock was ticking very quickly. Totally off subject, but I always wanted Mr Frosty the ice-making machine as a child, oh and Play-Doh barber shop! Anyway, back to the present, I thought.

I made an executive decision. Steven was going to have a shower so I thought I would fake a phone call to my mum from the room and as he came out the bathroom I would use my best acting skills yet again. He came out of the bathroom looking as gorgeous as ever with a crisp white towel wrapped around his waist, but I had to give my head a wobble and concentrate on the job in hand. I had the phone receiver in my hand and I started with the plan.

"Oh no, Mum, is everything okay?" I started in a startled manner. "Okay, I'll be home straight away, okay see you soon," and I hung up the blank phone call. I tried to look as sad and upset as possible.

"What's the matter?" Steven asked me, and he seemed really concerned.

"My Granddad has had a fall and I've got to get home asap" I relayed. "So, I won't be able to see you onto the train later, Im so sorry." I hated lying and one thing my mum always told me was that you had to have a good memory to be a good liar!

"Don't worry" Steven said as he came towards me and tried to hug me. He explained that family came first but I hated that I was letting him down blah blah.I also felt guilty about my dishonesty.

I put the last of my bits into my bag and zipped it up ready to leave to go seven doors down. I checked my watch, 11.20 so had to go right now, I'll deal with Steven later I thought but I had to see Joe, don't know why but I just had to.

Steven said he would call me later so that we could talk. As I left the room, I waited for him to close the door, and I walked quickly towards room 112. I glanced back quickly, just in case he decided to blow me a kiss as he usually did, but not this time. He knew I was still angry.

The door of Joes room was open as I got there and the cleaner's trolley was in the doorway. I double checked my watch 11.25. That's the right time I said to myself, trying to relay last night's conversation with Joe to make sure I hadn't got the time wrong.

I asked the cleaner where the lads were, and she shrugged and said, "checked out."

'Checked out!!! "How long ago?" I shouted to her. Once again, she shrugged her shoulders.

I ran to the lift as quick as I could and made my way to reception. I looked round the bar area and reception and Joe and his friends were nowhere to be seen. I walked as calm as I could to reception and the bloody same woman was working again, surely she had some time off I thought!

"Erm," I started. 'My friend in room 112 has checked out." She looked at me and started typing away on the reservation system.

"Sorry I can't divulge any information due to confidentiality."

Bloody jobsworth, didn't she know how important this information was. I wish she didn't have amnesia now! I ran towards the revolving doors.

Once outside I looked left and right and no sign. What was I going to do? I needed to see Joe, we hadn't even swapped numbers and I didn't know his surname. Note to self - Nicky, ask for surnames in future.

I needed to let him know how I felt. I stood there for a few seconds and realised I only had one option. Taxi to Lime Street station pronto.

Chapter 40

I FLAGGED THE first black taxi I saw and told the driver to get to Lime Street as quick as he could. God love the driver, he must have thought I was a tourist as he started going on about if I'd been to The Cavern, etc. I just nodded and pretended I was foreign and could not understand a word he was saying. The traffic seemed unusually busy, and the 10-minute journey was taking twice as long. Bloody road works everywhere. I was panicking, and I felt sick. My stomach was churning, and I was all flustered. I hadn't even brushed my hair. I quickly had a spray of perfume and a Polo mint. That will have to do.

Joe's train was leaving at 12.30, and by this time it was nearly 12.15. As we pulled up at the side entrance of the station by The Empire Theatre, I threw a five-pound note at the driver and ran out of the cab, not even shutting the door behind me. I ran in as fast as I could, trying to find the board that displayed the departures. There were stupid tourists and businessmen standing in my way as I dodged in and out, trying to get to the platform as quick as my legs would carry me. I found it at Platform 6, Newcastle Central. I was out of breath, and I ran and ran until I got there just in the nick of time. I saw him.

"Joe," I shouted "Joe," I shouted louder!

He turned round; he was just about to board the train. He dropped his bag and stood there. I ran towards him past the train guard who looked like he was about to blow his whistle to signal final boarding. I was like Zola Budd, I even impressed

The Wonder Bra Years

myself at my speed, even though I couldn't breathe. I ran into his arms, and he lifted me up off the floor, we kissed until I had to pull away as I needed gas and air!

"Where were you? "He asked.

"You left early" I replied. It did not matter now as I'd found him.

I had already written my phone number down on a piece of paper from the hotel, so I passed it on to him. "My number. Call me!" Joe's face lit up.

"Bloody right I will, I'll call you when I get home." I knew he would, I just knew. We kissed again until the guard called for the train to leave.

"Promise me you'll call," I begged.

"I don't need to promise pet, I'm not Steven, you know I will," and he gave me a wink and a smile. His smile lit up his face, looking into his eyes, I knew he would, I just knew because he wasn't Steven, and I had no doubts at all.

The whistle went, and the 12.30 to Newcastle Central pulled away from platform 6. I stood there still struggling to breathe, but I felt elated that I had seen him before he went. I think I was also shocked that the train was actually on time for once. I stood there for a few minutes mainly to get my breath together. I stood on the platform watching the train drive away slowly and into the dark tunnel at the end of the platform. I got myself sorted, wiped the tears from my eyes with my sleeve and turned to walk towards getting another bloody taxi. I had spent a fortune the last few days on bloody hackneys!

As I started to walk towards the entrance, I froze, and I mean I was frozen to the spot. Standing in front of me was Steven. What the hell was he doing here? Oh my god what was I going to say to him? I was supposed to be at home comforting my Mum because my Grandad had a fall! I had to think quick and think good. 1,2,3 here goes! And what if he had seen me with Joe?

"Oh, I've found you, I felt so guilty leaving you at the hotel, so I made a detour here, I needed to see you before you left, and I was hoping you would come to the station early and get a coffee or something because I had to leave." The lies just rolled off my tongue. I could tell he was suspicious, and I just hoped he hadn't seen me with Joe a few minutes earlier.

Steven looked at me in disbelief "Why are you here now then?" he enquired "You know my train wasn't till later" He was onto me big time I thought so I had to put my best convincing lovey-dovey Nicky act on.

The only thing I could think of at this time was to move towards him as seductively as I could, even though I was holding a Head holdall, hadn't washed my face and smelled of silk cut cigarettes, as I'd had at least three in the taxi journey from hell. I grabbed his face with my two hands and started kissing him in the sexiest style I could. I felt a bit embarrassed, but I needed to. Luckily, he accepted my advances, and we had the most amazing kiss, and I was not expecting it at all! Two amazing kisses in the last five minutes! Jesus, I will almost certainly get a cold sore this week sometime. This had almost certainly put a

The Wonder Bra Years

spanner in the works. I was more confused than ever. I thought my mind was made up about Joe about less than five minutes earlier, and now Steven seemed to have wormed his way back into my head yet again, after all, he was my number one, but he had given me doubts, and so far, Joe had an impeccable record.

Steven proceeded to tell me he had managed to swap his ticket for an earlier train etc. I looked like I was listening, but I didn't hear a thing. Mainly because I was still out of breath and secondly, I was so confused at the situation Id got myself into with him and Joe and was thinking of the next set of possible lies I may have to invent.

Steven told me his new train was leaving in half an hour, so he suggested getting a quick drink in the bar at the station. I felt rough as hell, so I thought another Bacardi might make me feel better, you know, hair of the dog and all that.

There was a bar upstairs in the main area of Lime Street. I always thought it looked a bit shady, so I had never been in or never had any reason to go in. We made our way there, and Steven went to the bar and ordered our usual round. I sat down, and he came over to the table with the drinks, and yes, he had got me a vodka and orange. The countdown until his train started, 20 minutes to go. I knew he was going to bring up our argument and the phone call that I hadn't heard a single thing about, but he didn't know that, and I knew there was something fishy about it.

"Please, Nicky," he started. "I promise there is nothing going on, and I'm not hiding anything"

He grabbed my hand and moved his chair closer to mine.

I was absolutely shattered and I was in no mood for a full meaningful conversation, well not at this precise moment but suddenly I felt this inner rage inside me and I decided to tell him what was on my mind. I had to get things off my chest for my own sanity. I could feel my face burning up as I started ranting. "Steven, you've let me down a few times now," and I gave him a look. "You stood me up on the last day of the holiday, didn't ring me for two days and then the phone call that I interrupted last night." I was on a roll! "Also, the phone number you gave me doesn't even exist. What am I supposed to think?"

He looked at me and lowered his head. "I know it looks bad," he replied, but I swear I haven't been dishonest with you. "It's just things that happen in everyday life, and it hasn't gone as well as we thought it would when we talked about things on holiday." It's too bloody true, I thought. It had been an almighty disaster so far. I grabbed my drink. No ice and no straw!! Terrible customer service I thought. Nevertheless, I had a big swig and it didn't have the desired effect. I thought I was going to throw up. Probably just topped me up from earlier on this morning.

Time was ticking as we chatted and then the station Tannoy announced that the Blackpool North train was leaving in five minutes from platform four. "You better get ready," I said to him as I finished the last bit of my drink and stood up. I looked at him, he looked broken but I had my self-preservation stance in full throttle and he needed to prove to me big time that he was

The Wonder Bra Years

serious about us if we were going to try and form some kind of relationship.

He stood up, grabbed his bag and followed me out of the bar and to the platform gate. I couldn't go onto this platform without a ticket, so we said our goodbyes at the turnstile.

"I promise I'll prove to you how much you mean to me, Nicky," he said.

At the same time, he put his two hands round my face and kissed me. "I'll call you tonight, I promise."

I kissed him back, and he walked away. He looked back at me and blew me a kiss. I wanted to catch it, but I had to turn away so that he wouldn't see the tears rolling down my face.

Chapter 41

YET AGAIN I found myself in another bloody black cab. I'm going to have to reign this in I thought. I'll have no money to spend in Wade Smith sale next week at this rate! Luckily, I wasn't at work today, so my plan was to get home, have a shower, and go to bed for most of the day. However, I was starving, so I needed food and a cup of tea first. My mum and dad were both in work thank God, I was not in the mood for explaining where I'd been and how my night was.

I got home, took my bag straight upstairs got changed into my pyjamas and then headed to the kitchen to find something to eat. First port of call was the fridge, nothing in there so next move the freezer. I spotted my favourite. Crispy pancakes! Minced beef and onion flavour my favourite. I lit the grill with the kitchen matches and placed three on the rack and got the tomato ketchup ready for the side. As they were cooking, I ran upstairs and had a quick shower as I felt disgusted. I put my PJs back on with my fluffy socks. I got back to the grill at the perfect time, just before the breadcrumb topping was about to catch fire and set the smoke alarm off. I got them out and onto a plate and added the ketchup. I wasn't in the mood for a brew because I was hungover and thirsty, so I got the Kia-Ora from the cupboard and made a pint of orange juice.

As the pancakes were cooling, I rang Sharon. As she answered, she had a bit of a kick-off because I had not spoken to her for a day or so, but once I explained what had happened

The Wonder Bra Years

with Steven booking the hotel, she let me off. She thought that was a nice gesture on Steven's behalf until I told her about his phone call. Id interrupted, and I knew she would have something to say about this. But before she had a chance, I told her the second part of the evening's events, and that soon shut her up when I told her about Joe and sleeping with him again. She went quiet.

"Are you still there? "I asked.

"Yes," she answered, and she started laughing uncontrollably for at least 30 seconds. "Oh Nicky" that's mad; I can't believe you left Steven in the room and went and shagged someone else a few doors down."

When I heard her relay to me what Id told her, it was my turn to go quiet.

"Nick, you Ok?" Sharon asked in a caring manner. No, I wasn't ok. What the hell had I done. This was a right bloody mess.

"Oh Sharon, what the hell have I done!" I started laughing too but I didn't know why probably nerves I thought. Steven was the one but there was something not right. Joe was gorgeous, funny, generous and he seemed loyal, but he wasn't my Steven. I had big decisions to make, but first crispy pancakes, cordial and bed. I wish the decision was as simple as who had the whitest reebok classics!

Sharon and I arranged to get together later. Either I would go to hers or vice versa. We will decide that later. For now, all I wanted was sleep and yet again, I was thankful I wasn't at work until tomorrow. As I lay down, I had awful stomach pains, the type that makes you double over with the pain. I probably needed a poo, especially after all the booze from this weekend. It must be my period, I thought. Hang on a minute, I should have been on by now, surely? I frantically looked for my date diary in my bedside cabinet but could not find it anywhere. I couldn't keep my eyes open, so I took two paracetamol and climbed into bed. I'll find it later, I thought.

I was awoken a few hours later by the neon blue light of my bedside phone ringing. I was half asleep as I answered and expected it to be Sharon sorting out our arrangements for later. She was so impatient at times!

"What do you want, nuisance? I'll be round later," I said in a groggy, half-asleep voice.

"Hello?"

It took me a few seconds to realise who I was talking to, and it was Steven. I was in double shock when I realised it was him, and I sat bolt upright in bed. "I've just got home," he said.

First thing that registered with me was it didn't seem like a phone box, no pips you see! "Oh Good" I mouthed back still half asleep.

"I told you I'd call you," he said.

I know he did but I half expected not to hear from him for a few days in his usual style. We chatted for ten minutes or so about this and that and I told him I was seeing Sharon later. He then brought up the subject of us getting together again next weekend. It was Sunday, and I couldn't even think further than teatime at this present moment, but I agreed to see him next weekend, and we would sort out the arrangements in the week. "Shall I come to you," I suggested? Blackpool wasn't far, and I fancied taking a trip.

"Err yeh, we will sort it out nearer the time," he replied; my mind was working overtime, and I was sure he was hesitant with his reply. I immediately decided this would be a deciding factor for me. If he put me off going to his house, then he would definitely be hiding something. Time will tell.

I lay back down when we had finished our call, and I was just lying there thinking about everything. I wouldn't be able to get back to sleep now so I rang Sharon and told her I'd be round in an hour or so and that I would pick up a bottle of wine or two and ten silk cut, or maybe twenty depending on what money I had left after all my taxi expenses over the weekend.

I jumped in the shower again for a quick freshen-up, and the phone started ringing again. Bloody hell, Sharon, I thought, what now? I picked up the receiver and started with my playful rant. "What now!" And started laughing.

"Hello, Pet. You ok?"

Shit, it was Joe! Well, if it doesn't rain, it bloody pours, I thought. "Hiya Joe, sorry, I thought you were my friend."

"I'm already missing you, Scouser," Joe laughed.

"Oh, bloody Nora," I thought to myself; this could only happen to me!

Chapter 42

It was lovely to speak to Joe; it had also been lovely speaking to Steven. Joe and I spoke for over half an hour. We were laughing and joking about the weekend. He was so easy to talk to.

"Have you spoken to him?" Joe asked? The tone of his voice changed slightly; I could tell he was a bit jealous. I'm a rubbish liar so I told him I had and that he had asked to see me at the weekend. "Oh well, I was going to suggest the same," Joe replied. Oh god, I didn't know what to do, so the only thing I could think of was to lie.

"Let me see what my rota is at work tomorrow for the weekend, and I'll let you know." It's the only thing I could think of, and I didn't think it was a bad lie, maybe a white lie, as I didn't actually know what shifts I was working until tomorrow until I got to work as the rota wasn't done until Monday Mornings. This seemed to pacify Joe for now, and he said he would call me the next day. The only thing I could think of was to speak to Sharon tonight and see what she suggested.

I threw my Dash tracksuit on with my Reebok trainers, a quick spray of Paloma Picasso from my mum's room for a change, and I called a village taxi. The operator said the usual 10 minutes, but I was ready, so I got my bits and bobs together along with the holiday photos from Max Spielman that I'd picked a couple of days before. I hadn't even had a proper chance to look at them with all the goings on of the last few days, so I was quite excited to see Sharon and have a drink and

The Wonder Bra Years

probably get pissed and reminisce about our holiday, which seemed like a lifetime ago. Sharon had also made me promise not to look at them until we were together. If I'd had the time, I would have definitely had a sneaky peak, but I hadn't.

I heard a beep outside from my taxi so I grabbed my bag and the photos and shut the front door behind me (Left the hall light on for security to make it look like someone was home, Dad's instructions engraved in my brain). I got in the taxi, and thankfully, it wasn't a leather gloveman; it was a young driver I'd seen before who was always chatty. I told him where I was going but via the off-licence at the top of my road. He pulled up on Rose Lane, and I ran into Thresher and grabbed two bottles of Liebfraumilch, a bottle of R whites' lemonade and twenty silk cuts. The driver, it turns out, was called John and was very chatty, and on the way to Sharon's in Aigburth, about 5 minutes away, he seemed more chatty than usual. Cut to the chase, he asked me out!! Ha, what is the actual? Tell you what men are like buses. All of a sudden, they all come at once. I told him I had a boyfriend; well, I suppose I had two half-boyfriends! If I had no one on the scene, I would have jumped at the chance, but there was no way I could handle another at the moment. I got out of the taxi and went outside Sharon's, and she was waiting at the door. "He's well fit," she exclaimed and laughed. I didn't have the energy to tell her he had asked me out; I just couldn't be bothered to explain. Plus, I had bigger things to discuss.

We walked into her back kitchen, and she already had two wine glasses ready. They were your typical wine glass shape but had different coloured stems. I had the blue one for Everton, and Sharon had the red one for Liverpool FC. The fact that we both supported different local teams wasn't an issue for us, but some families would have actual murder about their football team support, especially on Derby Day.

She took one bottle from me and proceeded to pour, and I put the other in the fridge. I sat down at the kitchen table and we both started perusing through the holiday photos. God knows what was on them, hopefully nothing rude and hopefully most would be in focus.

We grabbed a packet each and started screaming, laughing at the pictures of us, mainly drunk out of our minds, and unfortunately, quite a few were blurred and out of focus. I then came across one of me and Steven. I looked at them longingly. I placed the ones of us in a separate pile so I could keep them safe. The holiday seemed like a lifetime ago when I had no worries or doubts about Steven, and I hadn't even met Joe. Funny how things can change overnight. We drank, smoked and laughed, and on one occasion, I think I slightly pissed myself! I took myself to the toilet, half expecting my period to have reared its ugly head, but no, just wee. I must be constipated; I hadn't had a poo for days. My curiosity as to where my period was, came into my head again for the second time today, but I shrugged it off again; still too early for it, I thought and reminded myself to look for my little diary when I got home to check the dates.

Chapter 43

I WENT BACK downstairs to find Sharon laughing at our photos and the not so good standard of our photography skills on disposable cameras. I do not know why we bother with these as the pictures are always crap and I always used to forget to wind it on after taking a photo and it was never ready to take the next.

Sharon and I hadn't seen each other properly since the holiday so a good girly catch up and a giggle was what the doctor ordered. We finished the first bottle of wine and we both felt pissed. God knows how I did considering the amount of alcohol Id consumed recently. I should surely be almost immune by now.

We went through the six packs of photos and there were probably only about twenty pictures that were suitable for our parents to view and maybe another ten that were in focus. I mean there weren't any intimate pics apart from one of Stevens white arse that's Id taken on the sly one morning, well it was such a nice view I couldn't help myself.

The two bottles of wine went down far too easy last long so Sharon had a look in her mums' booze stash and found some vodka. Bloody Vodka again. There was no coke or fresh orange, so we had to settle for Tizer and I tell you what it was bloody lovely, went down a treat. As expected, we got quite drunk and the tunes came out. Sharon's Mum was at her Nans. Her dad didn't live with them anymore. Apparently, he had an affair with some "tart from work" Sharon's words not mine. As we were in holiday reminisce mood we put on one of the mix tapes that we took on holiday that I had brought with me. It was playing for a few songs until it decided to stop abruptly. The tape had tangled around the wheels of the tape deck on her mums Stack system so I took it out carefully and re wound it with one of my eyeliner pencils. Luckily I fixed it and there was no damage to her mums tape player. We were dancing and laughing and pissed as farts. The music was loud and it took us back to our carefree fortnight.

We sat down breathless from all the dancing and let a ciggie and had a shot of ouzo, also acquired from Sharon's mums' cabinet. I know it was a gift from our holiday but surely she wouldn't notice. She probably hated the stuff but it's all we could afford gift wise at the end of the two weeks. The shudder happened again and we both shook our heads in unison and laughed. We turned the music up and started dancing again. We hugged each other and told each other that we loved the other and we were best friends forever. You know the drunken conversation us girls have after a few drinks. We did mean it but you would never say anything like this sober. I've even told girls I have met in the toilet in The Hippodrome I loved them after talking to them for 5 minutes. I then started getting a bit emotional and told Sharon about the events of the last few days and the subsequent phone calls Id received earlier. I cannot believe I'd forgotten to tell her. We were too busy looking at the bright blue sea and the golden sand on our photos along with various pictures of feet and food and drinks we had consumed.

"Oh, he actually rang when he was supposed to," I said.

Sharon looked shocked. I was talking about Steven. I knew she didn't like him. She did in the beginning but when the let downs started mounting up her opinion had certainly been downgraded. Also the Ryan situation contributed to her dislike. She would be very different if her and Ryan were ok and she needed Steven and I to on good terms as well. Her views on the situation did not help me in the slightest

Next thing we heard a key in the front door and Sharon's mum Rita had arrived home from her Nans. Her arrival stopped me in my tracks as Rita made her way into the back room.

Sharon quickly kicked the alcohol cabinet shut with her foot and laughed at me and told me to shush. We quickly hid the empty vodka bottle under the table just in time. She took her coat off and came towards me and gave me a hug. She then sat down at the table with us as she noticed the holiday snaps. "Oh, and make me a brew please love while I have a nose at these," nodding to Sharon. Sharon obediently stood up and made her way to the kitchen.

"Let's have a look then, You look well Nicky you look like you've put some weight on, suits you. You were far too skinny" Rita said as she grabbed one of the photograph wallets.

Cheeky cow I thought but Rita did have the knack of speaking what she thought without thinking of the consequences. I remember one time she asked a girl in the local shop when the baby was due? She wasn't pregnant! My pants did feel a bit tighter come to think of it but the amount of crap and drinks I've had lately I'm not surprised I've put weight on. I'll have to find a new gym though. No way was I going back to The Moat House.

As we were so drunk I'd forgotten which wallet had the hidden ones in but I didn't care. Sharon re appeared with the cuppa and sat back down. Rita was commenting how lovely the views were on some photos, all 3 of them and then looked startled. "That's a nice view" she held it up for me to see and it was the one of Stevens bottom. I wanted to die. We all started laughing. I was starving so I suggested to Sharon we walk to the Chip shop at the top of her road. This suggestion went down well. We grabbed our jackets and made our way down the road to the local chippy. I had already decided I was getting chips fried rice and curry sauce. We got there just in time before they closed so the portion we got was huge.

We walked back down and immediately started to devour our naughty late-night treat.

I came over all tired, so I got Sharon to call my taxi while I carried on eating in my usual Olympic speed. It wasn't that late, just after 11pm but I was shattered and I had work tomorrow. I was still eating when I heard a beep outside so I wrapped up what food I had left in the white paper and got my stuff together.

I kissed Sharon and Joan goodbye and got into the taxi.

Oh, shit it was leather glove man!

Chapter 44

I GOT HOME safely from the clutches of leather glove man yet again! I walked in as quietly as I could, but you know what it is like when you are drunk. I knocked over a plant and fell up the stairs; so much for being quiet. I stripped off and got the PJs back on, and suddenly, I had awful tummy pains again. Bloody chippy food, no wonder she gave us loads, probably on the turn, obviously nothing to do with the wine, vodka and ouzo. I ran to the toilet as quick as I could, and I projectile vomited just in the nick of time. And pissed myself! I had no control over my bladder in these situations; God help me when I'm older! I kneeled in front of the toilet, waiting for the next wave to appear. It seemed to subside, so I bravely got up and made my way back to bed. Had to fish out clean pyjamas first as these ones were full of wee!! I couldn't find matching ones, but I didn't care, even though this usually irritated me.

I was never sick, and the rare time I was, it always ended in coming out both ends; my pelvic floor needed work for sure! By the time I cleaned myself up, it was just after midnight, and I needed my bed. I was on an early shift in the morning to set up the bar and restock the beer fridges. And I would also find out my rota for the weekend to see if I was working Saturday or not. To be honest, I wanted the manager to put me in all weekend so that it would make my decision easier and prevent me from seeing anyone. No time for such thoughts now; I needed my beauty sleep. A quick glass of water first, though.

My alarm went off at 8.00 am, and I snoozed at least 3 times. I eventually got up and made my way to the bathroom to perform my usual ablutions. I wasn't a high-maintenance girl, as I've mentioned before. After my bathroom duties, it was just a matter of brushing hair and putting bobble in, mascara and lipstick and a squirt of Anais Anais. Every time I picked up the white floral bottle, I thought of Steven and how happy I was on our flight home from Crete. As I went to leave the house again, my stomach started hurting again. I still hadn't had a poo, so I decided to get some laxatives from Boots on the way to work. It was then I remembered that I'd been sick last night. Bloody chippy has poisoned me, I thought! I tried to ignore the feeling and grabbed my stuff, made my way downstairs, grabbed my jacket and keys and started my usual walk to the bus stop.

The walk to the bus stop made me feel better; the fresh morning air felt nice on my face, and I started to feel better. I only had to wait a couple of minutes for the bus, and I decided to sit downstairs; I couldn't face going upstairs for a cigarette today or even being around anyone else who was smoking. The roads seemed quiet, so it didn't take long to get into town. I was due at work at 10.30, and I arrived on the dot. I always pride myself on my impeccable timekeeping. I hated people who were late, and that was Sharon all the time. I was always telling her off, but it fell on deaf ears. The manager was already there, so I said my usual pleasantries to him and had a brief chat regarding our day off yesterday and whether we had done

The Wonder Bra Years

anything interesting. I lied again. "Oh, lazy day and an early night."

I took my bag and jacket to the staff room downstairs, and on my way back upstairs to the bar, I had a glance in the manager's office to see if the rota for this week was done. Nope, not yet. It was usual practice to request specific days off at least a week before the required day. I started thinking about asking him for next Saturday off even though it was less than a week away, but something told me not to. My gut instinct yet again reared its ugly head.

I set the bar and dining area up. The tables were a mess from Saturday night, dead sticky so they needed an extra good wiping over. Before I knew it the manager came upstairs and opened the big wooden doors and placed the chalkboard outside with the list of cocktails and wines on offer.

Mondays were usually quiet, but today was a different story. It was quiet for the first hour, and then it was mad busy, with the usual people coming in for lunch or shoppers popping in for a cappuccino. I didn't even get my break until nearly 3.30pm. I'd asked the chef to make me my usual cheese and ham toastie with salad and chips. As I went downstairs to the kitchen, I grabbed my lunch and made my way to the staff room. I had a half-hour break, so after I'd eaten my food (5 minutes, you know me), I grabbed my bag and popped out to the kiosk around the corner to get ciggies and some chocolate. I got a Caramac and a Topic. I also popped into Boots and got some

Senokot. £3.00 robbing bastards. I lit a cigarette and walked back to work slowly so I could finish it.

I walked back downstairs to put my bag in the staff room, and on my way back upstairs, I noticed the rota was done and on the wall. I froze and walked towards it to get a closer look. My usual shifts were Monday, Tuesday, Wednesday, Thursday, Friday night, and Saturday, but this week's shifts were different. I was on evenings all week and Saturday!! This never happened never! As I was looking, the manager walked into the office, and I questioned him as to why my shifts were different. "Lisa is on holiday this week, love, so I've swapped you over and given you the weekend off; that's ok, isn't it?"

"Erm, yes, fine," I replied. He thanked me for being so flexible as I left the office.

Chapter 45

WELL, THIS HAD put a spanner in the works. I was off Saturday, so I could make plans to see Steven or Joe! Bloody hell, what was I going to do. I finished work at 5.00pm, so by the time I got home, it would be nearly 6pm. Steven said he would call me, and I said I'd call Joe! This was a right old mess. I decided to call Sharon as soon as I got in and ask her opinion. I mean, I know she would be Team Joe, but she knew how I felt about Steven.

As soon as 5pm came, I grabbed my stuff from the staff room and made my way to the bus stop. A few of the regulars who had become friends were drinking cocktails, and they asked me to join them. Usually, I would not hesitate for a second, but tonight, I had to get home even though I was dying for a drink. But I had my sensible Wurzel Gummidge head on for once and decided to go home and grab a bottle of wine from Thresher on the way home.

As I made my way to the Bubble bus stops, I picked up my wine, some salt and vinegar discos and some scampi fries. I waited about 5 minutes for my bus, and I started thinking what my plan of attack was tonight. First off, was to have a quick shower and put my none piss stained pyjamas on, open the wine and call Sharon for advice even though I half knew what she would say but still I wanted to discuss the new situation that I had been given.

Rachel Fegan

I was home just after 6pm and Mum was cooking the tea and it was one of my favourites, Liver bacon and onions with mash. She had the knack of cooking the liver so it was crispy and with the bacon and onions it was one of her specialties.
Dinner would be 10 minutes so I put the wine in the fridge and rushed up for a shower and change into my comfiest pjs. The smell drifted upstairs of my tea and I was downstairs as soon as I was dressed. I got the wine out and poured a glass for mum and I. Dad was in work till late so my intention was to save him a glass but that usually never came into fruition.

We sat on the sofa in front of the TV with our dinner on trays and started watching Granada Reports. I was eating and half-watching, but my mind was elsewhere. All I could think of was to ring Sharon as soon as possible before Steven called; well, that is, if he would go by his track record. Dinner was lovely. It was washed down with the Blue Nun wine, and Mum had Arctic Roll in for us for our pudding. I was trying to watch my weight after Rita's comments but thought, sod it, just this once wouldn't make a difference, surely? I'll start my diet tomorrow. Next minute the phone rang, my stomach turned and I quickly asked Mum to answer it and say I wasn't home from work yet and if it was Steven ask him to call back in half an hour. I just wasn't prepared for the conversation yet as I had not even had a chance to think about what I was going to do!

"1143." My mum answered the phone. Ha, she made me giggle when she answered the phone with our number. She was in the hall, so I stood at the door of the living room to listen to

The Wonder Bra Years

what was said. It was Steven. I could tell it was because she said it was nice to speak to you again. She gave the speech that I had asked her to give to me. I was still shocked that he had actually rang when he said he would. Maybe he had realised I would not stand for any nonsense. As soon as she placed the receiver down, I bombarded her with twenty questions, well, maybe five.

"What did he say? Was it Steven?" I started speaking so quickly that I didn't come up for air.

"I hate lying, Nicky; it's not nice. You wouldn't like it, would you"

No, I didn't, but this was an exceptional case. Mum started, "Yes, it was, and I said what you asked me even though you were listening, and he's going to call back in an hour; he sounds like a lovely boy." Good. I thought that would give me time to speak to Sharon and try to sort my head out. If I could, I could possibly phone Joe in the meantime. Lovely boy, ha! Well, I suppose he was, but his card was marked lately. Even though I didn't actually have any proof of any wrongdoing, I just knew there was something.

I ate my Arctic Roll with tons of ice magic on top and then made my way upstairs so I had some privacy on the phone in my room. I rang Sharon, but she wasn't even in! How dare she not be home when I needed guidance and urgently, too! I sat on my bed with my wine and lit a ciggie. I was allowed to smoke in my room if the window was open. My parents were good as long as the window was wide open and I didn't flick the stumps onto the conservatory roof. I don't know why they were so easy-going with me, but I suppose they thought she was going to do it anyway, so what's the point of kicking off. I decided I was going to be this easy-going with my kids if I ever had any. I didn't really like children. As I was an only child, I wasn't used to sibling rivalry, and I was quite grateful now because If I had a sister who stole my precious designer clothes, I would go bananas! When I was younger, I sometimes wished I had a brother or sister, but I was thankful now, and I did not know any difference.

The phone started ringing, and I answered, and thankfully it was Sharon. She started with the usual What did you have for your tea but I had to interrupt her and tell her about today's developments. Firstly, I told her about the rota news, and then I told her that Steven had actually called me, but I hadn't answered, etc. Sharon knew how much I liked or possibly loved Steven, but she didn't want to see me upset and hurt. We started with a pros and cons list for each boy. I grabbed a pad from my drawer and a novelty pen from Malia which, when you turned it, the man's clothes fell off and revealed his penis, childish but funny.

So, the list started. Pros for Steven, Fit, tall, sexy, good in bed, funny. Joe's pro list was the same! Well, this was not helping at all. The cons list was a lot different. Steven is unreliable, a suspect, and a liar; the phone is not working. Then I started Joe's Cons list, and it was blank, apart from a four-hour journey on a train to see him! If we added everything up, Joe would have come out as the winner, but Steven had this hold on my heart that would not go away. After 20 minutes of deliberating, we came up with a sort of decision for me.

If Steven insisted on coming to Liverpool and tried to put me off going to Blackpool, that would be the nail in the coffin for him, and I had a feeling this was what was going to happen. He had been dead cagey every time I mentioned going to his house, saying things like "The house is getting decorated, or we've got family coming over. Then I had to make my mind up whether to call Joe first now or wait for Steven to call back as his reply would seal the deal.

I decided on the latter, wait for Steven to call back and see what he had to say for himself.

Chapter 46

IT WAS GETTING on for 8.30pm, and Steven still had not rung back. To be honest, I wasn't surprised at all or remotely bothered, weirdly. I kind of expected it. The only thing I was conscious of was not calling Joe too late. I thought to sod it and started dialling Joe's number. I lit a cigarette and started keying in his number. My hand was shaking, and I felt nervous. As I finished dialling, the line went quiet, and for a moment, I had a feeling of Deja vu that I had when ringing Steven, and the line was dead. This time was different. The phone started ringing, and it wasn't long before Joe answered.

"What time do you call this Scouser?" He laughed. As soon as I heard his sexy Geordie accent, any nerves I had subsided. I told him a little white lie and said I had to stay on for an hour in work for an hour extra. We started chatting about our day, you know, the usual chit-chat before the elephant in the room was brought up. "So, have you got your rota?" He asked. I didn't know what to say. Obviously, I knew I was off on Saturday, but I hadn't made any decisions yet, especially as I hadn't spoken to Steven.

"I'll find out tomorrow; the manager was off today," I told another white lie! I'm going to go to hell, I thought to myself.

"Ok cool "he replied "I've already looked into a nice hotel for us and I've told my mum you might be coming up and she said she can't wait to meet you." Holy Shit I thought, he's told his mother about me! I just hope he hasn't told her everything about me, then again I couldn't remember most of it!

See this was the difference between Joe and Steven. Joe wore his heart on his sleeve and there were no mind games. Steven was like this at first then things changed or had I changed or was it just being on holiday made things seem so much easier. I longed to be back in Georgios apartments lying in bed with Steven making plans for the future. It was one of the happiest times I've ever had.

Joe and I were chatting for about an hour and the conversation just flowed, no awkward silences it was just lovely, everything I wanted or was it?

We eventually said our goodbyes, and I told Joe I was working the next evening. I nearly slipped up and mentioned my change in shifts but caught myself just in time. He didn't finish work till 5pm, so I told him I'd ring him on my break tomorrow evening. I thought I would use the phone in the manager's office. I looked at the time, and it was just after 9pm, I was tired, so I went downstairs and made a cup of tea, grabbed some biscuits and then got into bed and started reading Woman's Own, one of my Mum's magazines. I started doing a quiz: "Is he the one?" It is quite appropriate for me at the moment. It was one of those multiple choice quizzes where you picked A, B, C or D. Then you collated your answers and saw which letter you had the most. Mine was B. The result said, 'Don't try too hard if he's the one you will find out'.

What a load of shite! A total waste of ten minutes. I clock-watched, and it was nearly 10pm; he wouldn't be ringing now, surely. I always had a rule never to call anyone after 9, ideally, unless it was an emergency. This had given Joe extra points on his pros list. I know Steven had called me, and I dodged the call, but if you promise to call someone back, then you should. That's the way I saw things anyway. Chances are I won't speak to him tomorrow either, as I wasn't on my usual day shift that I had told him about. I put the magazine down the side of my bed and turned the ring off my phone. I got up and went to the bathroom, cleaned my teeth and washed my face, shouted goodnight to my Mum, shut my door and turned the light off. As I lay in bed, my stomach cramp returned, so I remembered I had bought the Senokot. I fished the packet out of my bag and quickly read over the instructions. It said to take two tablets at night for morning relief. I took two tablets out and took them with some water from last night. They tasted nasty. Hopefully, they would work in the morning as I was sick of the pain and was desperate for the toilet.

I was tossing and turning for a while, thinking about Joe and how kind he was and then Steven, who was so unpredictable. One minute, he seemed to be making headway, making up for letting me down, and the next, he was back to square one in the doghouse. He probably fell asleep, I told myself, yes, that's it. I set my alarm for 10am. It was nice to lie in unless my bowels woke me up sooner. I didn't know what I was going to do with myself before work tomorrow; I shall decide in the morning. This was a novelty to me since I was off work during the day, and I wasn't sure if I liked it.

Chapter 47

I WOKE UP before my alarm at about 9.00am. The sun was shining through my window right onto my bloody face, and I felt sad that it wasn't the sun from Crete. I lay there for a bit, trying to decide what to do with myself. The next minute, my stomach started to make gurgling noises, and I had the urge to go to the toilet. I stood up and grabbed the magazine from the side of my bed to take with me just in case it was a while. I had been on the toilet for ages once I had started reading a copy of my dad's Reader's Digest that he had left behind the radiator in the bathroom, and this was the most boring thing I'd ever read. I would rather read the ingredients of the Bleach from the side of the toilet.

I sat on the loo opened the magazine and then timber! Good lord the laxatives had definitely worked. Afterwards I felt like I had lost about a stone! No need to diet now I thought.

I had noticed yesterday there were some sales on in town so I decided to have a lazy morning and then leave the house a couple of hours before I was due in work so I could have a browse round the sales. I went downstairs and made a coffee and some toast and took it back upstairs and got back into bed. I felt so much better after going to the loo. Like a new woman.

For one moment I thought about calling Stevens number just to see if it rang. As much as I wanted to believe him the trust had been broken. I didn't call, I didn't want to know if I'm honest.

I sat up in bed as I still didn't feel 100% even after earlier. It was then that it dawned on me that I still hadn't come on my period. I opened my bedside drawer and shuffled round all the shite that was in there. I found my date diary and proceeded to find today's date. I didn't even know what date it was.

I was due three days ago. I wasn't too concerned as I was never as regular as clockwork.

I always had to give or take a few days either side.

I rang Sharon and thankfully she answered. I needed to speak to her and this wasn't the type of conversation that could be done over the phone so I asked her if I could pop round to see her before work. Sharon had had a few scares in the last twelve months but thankfully it all ended up ok.

Luckily, she was free today, so I told her I'd be around at lunchtime. She said she'd make me a cheese toastie for my lunch. That is why she was my best friend, always thinking of me in weird and wonderful ways. I said thank you, but because of how I was feeling at the moment, I couldn't eat anything.

I started to run a nice bath with plenty of bubbles. As I was running, I shaved my legs and armpits. I didn't do down below, just in case I needed to be all smart for the weekend. I got into the hot bath and submerged my whole body under the warm water. I lay there thinking. Thinking about everything, especially the situation of the missing period. I know it wasn't that late, but I couldn't help but worry. I kept going through the past few weeks in my mind with Steven and Joe. I had been careful with Steven apart from that last time on holiday and Joe!

Well, I didn't remember a single thing of the first night, so God knows if I'd been careful or not and the second time, shit!

Oh lord this was getting worse. I couldn't wait to tell Sharon for her to give me reassurance but then I didn't want to tell Sharon as I felt like a bloody idiot. I think for the first time ever she might actually be speechless.

After my bath I got ready into my work clothes because at this point I still had the intention to go clothes shopping after I'd been to Sharon's. Quick spray of deodorant and the usual make up ritual and I was ready to leave. I decided on getting the bus as it was such a nice day and Id save money instead of getting another bloody taxi, plus the fact I was not in the mood for leather glove man!

I walked up the road and popped into the corner shop for some ciggies. As I walked out of the shop, I opened the packet and lit one up. It was then a sudden thought came into my head of the risks of smoking when pregnant. What the hell was going through my head. It was mad. I did not even know if I was pregnant or not, and if I was, would I even keep it? These thoughts kept going through my mind.

The bus came, and I sat downstairs, where there were only a few stops. I stared out of the window, dazed, and before I knew it, my stop was here. Sharon's house was a five-minute walk away from the bus stop. As I turned into her road, she was on the step talking to her neighbour. I said hello to the neighbour and followed Sharon inside. We sat in the kitchen, and she put the kettle on. She had started the preparation of my toastie; it just needed to be put on the Breville toastie machine. She placed my mug of tea in front of me and sat down next to me. I did not want to make any small talk, and I was too anxious. I just came right out with it.

"Right, I'm in a bit of a pickle," I started.

"What!" She laughed. "Have you shagged someone else last night?" We both started laughing. I wish it was as easy as that I thought.

I didn't know how to start explaining, so I just blurted it out. "My period is three days late," I exclaimed.

As expected, Sharon was lost for words. She stared at me open-mouthed for a good 30 seconds or more. "Say that again," she muttered, almost stuttering her words. I repeated my statement, and it had the same effect as the first time.

"Nicky, what!" Sharon started, and she stared straight into my eyes. "You're always the one preaching to me to take precautions."

"I know," I started. "I thought I had. That's what I don't understand." I did understand. I had taken at least two chances unprotected with two different people, but I felt a bit embarrassed about this, so I decided not to divulge this information to her even though she probably knew anyway. I decided to keep this fact to myself as it didn't really make a single bit of difference now did it.

After an extremely awkward silence, Sharon started to work on her agenda. "I'm sure you will be fine, it's only three days.

Remember that time? I was nearly two weeks late, and I was ok. If it makes you feel better, why don't you get a test."

I had already thought about this, but I didn't want to face the truth about what this would mean to me, how things would change and what the hell would my Mum and Dad say. Also, I was skint until payday, so I couldn't afford a Pregnancy test as I needed money for wine and ciggies.

In the meantime, Sharon had done my toastie and served it up with a glass of Dandelion and Burdock from the Alpine delivery man. I struggled to eat one-half, but I managed just about it. The fizzy drink was nice and gave me a nice sugar boost. Sharon could tell I was worried, so she changed the subject and asked me about the weekend and if I had made any decision. I told her about Steven calling and telling my Mum to lie for me, and the fact that he didn't call back. I then told her about the conversation with Joe and how lovely he was, and that he had told his Mum about me.

Well, you can guess what Sharon's response was. Team Joe all the way.

Chapter 48

I LEFT SHARON'S just after 2pm and walked up her road towards Aigburth Road to get the bus into town. There were always plenty of buses available on this route, so I didn't have to wait long. I sat downstairs again as the thought of smoking or even the smell of it knocked me sick at the moment. This wasn't like me; I loved a ciggy on the way to work. Shit, I hope this isn't one of those pregnancy symptoms you read about!

I got into town just before 3pm and got off at Lewis's. This was the usual point that we got off the bus and it was a central meeting place for most people, under the Dickie Lewis statue that was above one of the main doors of the shop. It was a statue of a man with his arm in the air and his willy and balls on show! Quite rude, God knows how it got commissioned!

Lewis's had a few fashion concession stores all under one roof so it was always a good first port of call. I had about £50 quid to spend that had to last me until payday but I needed retail therapy to take my mind off things. My heart just wasn't in it. I kept thinking about pregnancy tests and everywhere I looked I could see children running round and stressed out looking mums with crying kids in prams drinking tea out of a bottle.

Nothing caught my eye there, so I made my way up to Church Street to Miss Selfridge, Kookai and Oasis; they always had good sales. I did fancy a new pair of going-out shoes, so I also wanted to check out Ravel and Saxone. I wandered into

Miss Selfridge and saw a nice black bodysuit with frills on the shoulders. Bodysuits were a pain on a night out, though when you were pissed, trying to re-attach the poppers drunk nearly always ended up in a pubic hair catchment disaster or piss drips. So ladylike, I know, but facts are facts.

I bought the bodysuit for £7.00, reduced from £25.00, so that was my first bargain. I wanted shoes next, so I made my way to Ravel. On the way there, I walked past a couple who were smoking, and the smell knocked me sick. I wasn't going to vomit, but the feeling that rushed through me was awful. I sat on a bench in the street for a few minutes to sort myself out. The feeling soon subsided, but I had lost all interest in shopping. All I could think of was going to Boots for a test. I didn't want to do it, but I had to know if I was or wasn't. I could be panicking over nothing, and if I did the test, at least I could relax if it was negative.

There was no or. It had to be negative. I did not know what I would do if it was positive.

I headed towards the blue Boots sign and made my way toward the aisles that sold the tampons and sanitary towels; quite ironic, really. How I wish I was coming in here to buy Body form. I walked towards the pregnancy tests. I was looking over my shoulder the whole time in case I saw anyone I knew. Imagine the rumours if anyone saw me buying a First Response test. There were a few different tests on the shelf, so I grabbed the test, placed it in my palm, turned my hand around, and made my way to the cashier. I handed it over, paid, and put it in my bag as quickly as I could. I didn't even look at the price; I just handed the cashier ten pounds and put the change in my pocket.

I had no clue what to do with it as I had never done one before, so I put it to the back of my mind till later. Sharon will know, as she has done a few lately. Right now, I was feeling better for a change, and I still had an hour before I was due to start work, so I went on mission shoe shopping. I walked back towards Dolcis, which had a big sale sign in the window. I walked in and went to the sale rack. I had size 7 feet, so there were usually a few in my size. A pair of black sling-back kitten heels caught my eye, so I tried the one on the rack. It looked nice, so I got the other from the sales assistant. I had no energy to try the other one on, so I went straight to the cash desk. The cashier tried to sell me the usual leather protector spray, but I politely declined. I handed her a tenner; they were £9.99, reduced from £29.99. I was usually euphoric when I'd got a bargain, but today, I did not feel like celebrating. My mind was elsewhere. I still had 45 minutes before work, so I popped into Wimpy for a coffee and a ciggie.

After I got my drink, I sat down and carefully got the leaflet with instructions for the pregnancy test. I read it, and I gathered the main jist of it was to perform the test first thing in the morning when your urine had the most pregnancy hormone in. Right, I told myself I would do it at home in the morning when Mum and Dad were both at work. My nerves were shot. What was I going to do if it was positive?

Chapter 49

I WALKED IN the front door of Labellos, and it was absolutely rammed. This was unusual for a Tuesday. I found out from Claire that there was a leaving do-in for one of the makeup sales assistants from the local Department Store, George Henry Lee. These girls came in quite often for lunch, and they always looked glamorous, and their makeup was always spot on. I was shit at makeup. I'd only started using foundation in the last few months. I only usually went for mascara and some lippy. I did the usual staff room regime and reapplied my lipstick, brushed my fringe, sprayed some Insette and made my way to the bar.

The hours of 5pm and 7pm were Cocktail Hours, and the cocktails on the menu were £1.99 instead of the usual price. This inevitably meant that it was dead busy, with everyone wanting to get pissed for a tenner. The cocktails were straightforward to make, and after a few busy nights, the recipes for the Long Island Iced Tea and the Multiple Orgasm became second nature.

I was conscious that I promised to ring Joe on my break, which would probably be about 8pm. I had also decided I would call home and ask my mum if Steven had called back first. I decided to myself that if Steven hadn't called back, I was going to make plans to see Joe at the weekend. My break eventually came after 8.30 when the bar had quietened down, and the food orders had stopped. Luckily, the manager popped out at the same time to go to the pub over the road for a drink with the manager of the bar next door, so I went to the office and called Mum. To cut a long story short, Steven had not called. I was so disappointed. I really thought he would have, seeing as he promised to call back last night. Right, my mind was made up, and I proceeded to dial Joe's number. It was ringing for what seemed like ages, and I was about to hang up when a woman answered the phone. This put me off my stride. I assumed Joe would answer, seeing as he was expecting my call. "Erm, hello, can I speak to Joe, please?" I said nervously.

"Is that you, Nicky Pet?" Answered a soft-spoken lady.

"Yes, hiya," I replied.

"I'll just get him for you, love, see you soon, I've heard all about you."

Aww, she seemed so sweet, and what was even more sweet was the fact that Joe must have spoken about me quite a lot to his mum. I heard her shout Joe in an extremely loud voice, not so soft spoken now, I thought. This is something my mum would do.

"Hello, scouser," Joe said "You Ok? I hope you have got good news for me about the weekend."

Did I? Shall I commit to going to Newcastle, or did I wait to speak to Steven? It took me all of 2 seconds to answer him. "Yes, I have Pet," I giggled as I answered. I told him I had Saturday off, and he was ecstatic. He then told me he had already booked a guest house in the town centre, but he also told me that his mum had said I was very welcome to stay at their house. He left that decision with me to think about. He had also investigated the train times from Lime Street to Newcastle Central. The earliest one was 8am Saturday morning, and it would take about four and a half hours as there was a change at Preston or something. I wasn't too sure about staying at his mum's house even though she seemed lovely, but the whole point of seeing him was to have a sexy time, and the states I got in, god knows what I was going to do. Probably went somewhere inappropriate and had noisy sex with her son.

"I'll send you a cheque in the post for your train fare," Joe offered. "Or I'll give you the money when you get here." Could he get any better?

"It's Ok, I'll pay. You can take me out in the night," I replied. I hated being reliant on a man for money, but I expected them to pay for most of it.

"Deal," he laughed. I had ten minutes of my break left, and I wanted a quick sandwich and a ciggie, so I said my goodbyes. We planned to speak again tomorrow at the same time. I actually told Joe about my shift changes, so he understood if I was a bit late calling him.

My curiosity got the better of me, so I quickly rang my mum back to see if there were any developments. There were. Steven had called; it must have been about a minute after I called Mum earlier. She told him I was at work, so he left a message for me to call him tomorrow afternoon as he was on a half day. I hung up the phone and sat on the manager's twirly chair. I had a spin around a few times, thinking as I went round and round. There must be a full moon or something. You couldn't make this up.

The Wonder Bra Years

I went into the kitchen and grabbed my tuna mayonnaise baguette from the side and stuffed some of it into my mouth and walked towards the staff room to grab my fags. I had half the sandwich and then lit my cigarette. I inhaled it and blew the smoke out with a sigh. A very loud sigh.

The end of my break came, and I made my way back upstairs. The bar had gone a lot quieter, and I was secretly hoping it would stay like this so the manager would close early. My wish came true luckily and we closed at 10.30pm. I usually got a taxi home, but tonight I fancied fresh air, so I thought I would get the bus. To be honest, I felt like walking. Just walking around town with just the glow of the streetlights and a weird sense of quietness with the odd drunk person here and there. I had so much on my mind and knew I couldn't sleep just yet. I contemplated getting some wine but decided not to as I had drank so much lately, and my skin looked shocking; I was even getting spots again. No way I was starting on the Clearasil again. I walked for a while, just the distance of two bus stops. I got by Lewis's as I had earlier in the day.

I sat on the bus stop plastic bench and lit a cigarette. Just as I finished and stood on it like Olivia Newton John the bus arrived to take me home. I had a lot to think about tomorrow, things I did not really want to think about but I had to, I had no choice.

Chapter 50

I WOKE UP before my alarm because of the bloody sun shining through my curtains again. Id decided I didn't like doing the evening shifts. I hated having to hang around all day waiting to go to work, I couldn't relax properly. Also, the fact that I might be pregnant and I did not know who the father was. Ill end up on The Kilroy show at this rate.

I had decided I was going to call Steven just after lunchtime. I knew he said he would be home, but I thought I would leave a message and explain that I was on the evening shift most of the week to cover staff holidays. I don't know why I was so bothered. Even though he had rung last night, he did not ring back the night before, and if he had, I could have thought about the weekend plans differently, but he might have a decent explanation for this. I am always falling asleep after work. I'm sure I have got a touch of Narcolepsy.

I went downstairs, made a coffee, and put two crumpets in the toaster. I sat on the sofa for a few minutes, waiting for the toaster to pop, so I started reading some of my mum's magazines again. Take a Break was on the coffee table, so I had a quick glance, but they had nothing of interest to me. At least my More magazine had juicy stuff in, but I did have a quick glance at the top tips in Take a Break. These made me laugh. The fact that people wrote in with this crap baffled me. "If you are hosting a dinner party and don't have spare cash, simply make after-dinner mints by freezing a tube of toothpaste and cutting them into wafer-thin slices and serving on a decorative plate" Ha-ha, the tears were rolling down my face, cheered me, up no end. The toaster had popped, so I put my usual butter and lemon curd on them and started eating them until a wave of sickness reared its ugly head.

I thought I'd have to do this bloody test. I wanted to know, but I didn't at the same time. This was such a life-altering thing, and I did not have the courage to face up to it yet. I made an executive decision. I will enjoy one last weekend. I will try to take it a bit easy, just in case, and then, on Monday morning, I will face up to it and do the test. Hopefully, my period would come before then, but I didn't want to be on my period if I was going to see Joe. Good god, Nicky, I thought you have got a cheek! One minute, you want a period; the next, you don't!

I remembered the message from my mum to call Steven in the afternoon. I waited until just after 12pm and I went into the hallway and sat on the bottom stair and started dialling his number. Steven had told me the phone was fixed now so I dialled the number and hoped it wasn't another lie.

After a couple of seconds of silence, it started ringing and a girl answered and this threw me totally.

"Hiya, can I speak to Steven, please?" I asked in my poshest voice.

"Who's calling?" the girl asked in quite a stand-offish manner.

"It's Nicky."

There was a silence, a very awkward silence.

"He's at work" she replied.

"Thank you. Can you tell him I called, please?"

Before I could finish, the girl hung up. I still had hold of the phone with the continuous tone in my ear. Who the hell was that? It certainly was not his mum. She sounded well too young, and he hadn't mentioned a sister or had he. My memory was so bad, especially when I was pissed.

As usual after a phone call like this I just sat on the bottom stair for a few minutes or so collecting my thoughts. My first thought was to call Sharon but she was in work today, bugger. All kinds of scenarios were going through my head, mostly negative ones, yet again.

I wasn't due for work until 4pm today and didn't know what to do with myself; it was only 12.15pm. If I sat around, all I would do was mope about thinking the worst. I did consider going to the gym, but that thought soon passed. I couldn't show my face in that gym ever again. There was only one other option, more retail therapy. The first thing on my agenda was a nice hot shower, washing my hair and making myself look half decent even though I just wanted to curl up in a ball and cry and listen to sad songs on the radio. Sometimes, late at night, I'd put the radio on and listen to the Peaceful Hour on Radio City. It ran from midnight for an hour every evening and had requests from lovers or people like me who were sad and wanted a good old cry.

I got undressed and got into the shower. I couldn't find my mum's posh stuff; she must have hidden it as I'd been using it

The Wonder Bra Years

quite a lot. I'd even topped it up with water and given it a good shake, hoping she wouldn't notice. No good stuff handy, so I had to use the remnants of a bottle of Matey from about five years ago that I had got in my Christmas Stocking for a laugh off my dad. Yes, I still have a Christmas stocking. Even at this age, I started feeling a bit sick again. I wasn't going to be sick, but the feeling was awful. I thought about doing the test just so I would know, but I just could not bring myself to. Selfishly because I wanted one more weekend getting pissed and smoking, I still had about 300 ciggies left from holiday. If I knew I was pregnant, there was no way I'd drink or smoke even though I had not even decided If I would go ahead with it. A girl I went to school with had had an abortion, or so the rumour had it.

I wasn't religious about the whole abortion issue, but it was something I had never had to think about before. I had gone into another trance thinking about the what ifs that I nearly passed out in the hot shower. I washed my hair and eventually got out because I was having a hot flush. I just hoped it was the temperature of the water and not another possible pregnancy symptom.

Chapter 51

I DECIDED TO doll myself up today. I felt like I needed to look attractive; God knows why I needed to boost my self-confidence. I was feeling sorry for myself. The phone call to Steven earlier was playing on my mind, along with the obvious. Who was that girl? And where was Steven? He was meant to be off today. I was thinking about calling back because I had rung him quite early in the afternoon, and I wanted to know who the girl who had answered my call was. I blew dry my hair and went over it with my BaByliss hair straighteners. I used to have the crimpers, too, but I am way too cool for crimped hair these days. I made it as sleek as I could, but when you have naturally curly hair like mine, it makes the job a lot tougher. Next was my make-up.

As I have said before, I wasn't a big make-up girl unless I was going out. Rather than the usual azure blue mascara for a night out, I used a black/brown one from my Mum's make-up bag. I had hair mascara, too, which looked cool; I was tempted to put a few streaks in but thought better of it. Save that for the weekend, maybe. So, it was foundation, Arabian glow and my Rimmel Heather shimmer lipstick with a layer of lip cote on the top. Not that I'd be snogging anyone; well, you never know with me lately.

I got dressed for work and stood in front of the full-length mirror inside my wardrobe door. If I do say so myself, I look half decent. I stood sideways and looked at my stomach. Was that a bulge, or was it wind? I gave my head a wobble. Shut up, Nicky. I thought you being stupid now. This whole situation has been affecting every aspect of my life lately. I knew that taking the test would give me the answer, but I just couldn't bring myself to do it; I was too scared. It would be different if I was in a committed relationship or a bit older, but I wasn't in either. I was a stupid teenager who had let her heart rule her head and had made stupid choices when drunk. I knew I wouldn't be the first girl to feel like this, and I definitely wouldn't be the last.

Time seemed to stand still today. I checked the clock radio by the side of my bed, and it was only just after 1pm. I was good at shopping, but I wasn't in the mood for four hours of traipsing around the sales that mostly consisted of shite left from last year or ridiculous items that I wouldn't seem dead in; well, it depended on the price. I kept thinking about calling Steven back, but I was too scared. I left a message with "her," so I just hoped she passed the message on.

I left home just before 1.30pm and leisurely strolled up to Allerton Road to get the bus. I got on the first bus into town. I sat upstairs and lit a ciggie. After a few stops, one of my friends, who I used to go to school with, got on. She was one of those girls who always seemed to be lucky, always had the latest fashion, and was always a hit with the boys. I secretly hated her, but I put my best friendly Wurzel Gummidge head on. We had all grown up now.

I was shocked when she walked towards me, she looked awful, not at all like she used to look in school. She recognised me as soon as she walked towards me and she sat on the double seat in front We said our pleasantries to each other and started chatting. Her name was Jane. She was more like plain Jane now.

We started chatting about this and that and she started telling me that she had a baby. My ears immediately pricked up and I was curious as to what had happened and how her life was now. If I could have out a bet on anyone going to university and having an amazing life it would have been her. I was quite shocked. I couldn't believe what I was hearing.

She started telling me all about it. She talked about the sleepless nights, the stretchmarks she couldn't get rid of and the fact that she had no life anymore. Her partner had left her when he found out she was pregnant, and his parents practically disowned her while she was pregnant, but they came around when her son Joshua was born. He was 18 months old, and she did seem happy being a mum, saying that it was all worth it when he giggled or smiled at her; she even showed me a Polaroid photograph of him. He was so cute, but you could tell by her appearance that she didn't look like the girl she used to be. Her usually perfectly dyed blond hair had brown roots, and she looked exhausted. Something inside me was dying to tell her my predicament, but there was no way I was going to tell anyone. I wasn't even sure I would tell Sharon. I know that sounds awful, but this is something I would sort out on my own if I could. Anyway, I'm probably worrying about nothing.

This gave me things to think about. I did not even think about what I'd say to Steven or Joe if the result was positive. And how could I tell who was the father? This was getting worse by the minute. For God's sake, you stupid monthly pain in the arse, make an appearance, will you please!

As Janes's stop came close, she offered me her phone number and asked if I fancied keeping in touch? Usually, I would have accepted and had no intention of keeping in touch, but seeing as I may be in a similar position to her, I gladly accepted it and promised to call her, and I meant it. I might just need some advice very soon. Just shows you how appearances can be deceptive. She was really nice, totally different than she was in school, but I suppose having a baby made you grow up in more ways than one. She did give me quite a lot to think about.

The main thing that was playing on my mind was abortion, so I decided to investigate this, just in case. I didn't know where to start looking, so I assumed it was the Yellow Pages. I knew a girl who had one. Well, that was the rumour, but this wasn't the type of thing I wanted to ask anyone just in case it wasn't true; abortion was still quite a taboo subject. The only thing I'd really thought about was not being able to drink and smoke; totally selfish, I know, but I loved my carefree life, and I doubted whether I was ready to give it all up.

As I sat there looking out of the window, I decided I was going to do the pregnancy test first thing in the morning. I was not going to have "one more weekend".

I was going to be responsible and find out once and for all what lay ahead, and whatever it was, I would deal with it as I knew I could.

Printed in Dunstable, United Kingdom